THE WILLISTON EXPERIENCE

A Story of Boomtown Greed

WILLIAM H. SCHMALTZ

TheWillistonExperience.com

RIVER'S BEND PRESS
2015

The Williston Experience: A Story of Boomtown Greed

First Edition

ISBN – 978-1-935607-16-8

Published by River's Bend Press
Post Office Box 606
Stillwater, Minnesota 55082 USA
www.riversbendpress.com

Illustrations by Daniel Belic
- http://daniel-belic.deviantart.com

Library of Congress Cataloging-in-Publication Data
Schmaltz, William H.
The Williston experience : a story of boomtown greed / by William H. Schmaltz. – First edition.
pages ; cm

ISBN 978-1-935607-16-8 (softcover : acid-free paper)

I. Title.

PS3619.C4427W55 2015

813'.6—dc23

2015003613

Acknowledgements

Many people inspired this novel. Some friendly, some not-so-friendly. Each person taught me things about their nature and their world view. Their personalities are in this novel.

This novel is dedicated to the living. Go out and create something, anything, in tribute to those who have inspired you and those who continue to inspire you.

As always, special thanks to my family - my wife Natalie, my children - Henry, Molly, Karl.

-whs

2015
Las Vegas, Nevada

CHAPTER I

"Fuck the government!"

"Fuck - the - government," Wayne yelled again.

Wayne Carmack was bored and agitated by his thoughts. He switched off the radio. Tom Petty's nasal whining was iritating him. The CD player in his piece-of-shit Chevy Blazer was broken, so he was forced to listen to *commercial radio.*

Matrix radio.

Wayne had it all figured out. Radio and television were tools – the modern delivery method for manipulating the masses; shaping their tastes, their wants, their desires – so the lemmings would buy *their* products.

Corporations concocted radio playlists for every sector of the human population. In time, the playlists were like bad college professors – you just couldn't get rid of them. The Corporate Controllers were attempting to sell *another generation* of youth the same music they had sold their parents—and it was working. The same music in every state – from Seattle to Miami – a giant monolithic music list, rolled out like a soft blanket over the entire map. So soft and smooth that most people never noticed it. The same people who watched unmuted commercials on their TV's, accepted and embraced whatever music came out of the radio.

This strategy worked well with White people; the TV-addicted, fast-food eating robots who are so easily controlled, but not so well with Black people. Blacks have a history of rejecting White man's music; they weren't included in White society; why the hell should they listen to White man's music? They invented their own music – and made fortunes along the way by *ignoring* the White man.

The way forward was to reject the corporate creations. The power and control of the corporation was vast, but not supreme. You could beat it, by rejecting it; the Black man had proven it. Wayne didn't understand their music but he was awed by their ability to carve out something new – and give Whitey the middle finger while doing it.

The Chevy Blazer was all he had left after getting fucked-over by the state of Minnesota on his child support. What remained of his savings account had been spent on the 1967 Arrow "can-of-ham" trailer, towed behind the Blazer.

His divorce decree burned his ass. Eleven-hundred a month in child support for one kid – while the ex-wife made $85,000 a year on a *government* job. He tried the appeal process; he tried reasoning with the bureaucrats about the unfairness of the decree.

Why should he be mandated to live at poverty levels why that bitch got to live high-on-the-hog with his tax-free income?

Nobody in the system gave a "rats' ass" about the inequities of the system. The woman judge in particular, enjoyed the fact that there was such a nasty disparity. "I don't make the laws Mr. Carmack," she had said with a smirk.

"It is what it is," his friend Larry would say.

Wayne glanced over at Larry, sleeping in the back seat. A budding alcoholic, Larry had drunk most of their cooler of beer the previous night. It was Wayne's turn to drive; he didn't mind Larry sleeping it off. He liked to be alone with his thoughts anyway.

It bothered him that Larry made life look so easy. Larry rolled with life, like it didn't matter. Larry got fucked-over by the court on his divorce too, but he didn't care. He didn't *expect* any justice in life; he lived each day with a smile on his face, not a care in the world.

That's idiotic. You should live fired-up and pissed-off.

He looked out the window at the vast flat prairie of North Dakota. It wasn't ugly like Detroit or Houston, but it wasn't beautiful like Wyoming or Montana.

A flat wasteland of nothing; like the surface of Mars with grass.

It went on and on as far as he could see. The drive from Minneapolis was taking longer than expected. The monotonous plains were starting to get to him. He reached into the back seat, flipped open the cooler and took out one of the last bottles of beer. He glanced at his watch. It was 7:00 a.m.

Beer-thirty in North Dakota. Fuck the Law.

He raised it to his lips, took a long draw, and thought about his new life in Williston.

~~~

The lights of the Denver skyline receded to just
~~~

a twinkle in the rear view mirror of Lisa Wagner's Volkswagen Jetta – the "Nazi-wagon" as her last boyfriend called it. He was an asshole; like most of the men in her life. At 26 years old, she gave up on finding *Mr. Right*, *the One*, or the horrid-sounding, *Soul Mate.*

Not gonna happen.

Those ideas were fairy-tales, created and perpetuated by the media and delusional mothers—such things *do not exist in real life.*

She'd been through so many relationships. The ups and downs, the fighting, negotiating, the narcissism – she couldn't do it any more, she was burned out. She didn't like being single; it was a lonely path through life, but it was better than the depressing, drama-filled relationships she'd been in.

Pole-dancing didn't make things any easier. The money was great; way better than waitressing or bartending.

Four years in college and a worthless bachelor's degree in Art History.

Her first post-college job as a secretary paid $12 per hour.

Barely enough to pay rent and gas, let alone the fucking student loans.

Her mother told her the student loans had to get paid off; they couldn't be discharged in bankruptcy court like a typical loan. Mother had co-signed the loan, so they *had to get paid off.*

Lisa read on *ContraCorner* how the bankers and bureaucrats in Washington and New York had rigged it. The little people were under the heel of the boot, rules and regulations, chase-you-to-your-grave wealth confiscation, while the crooked-bankers received Congressional bailout when *they* messed up.

She took great care of her curvy, vegan-body with yoga and health club routines. The strip-club men appreciated it too; they covered the floor around her pole with greenbacks—the more she teased them—looked them in the eyes, the more they fell in love with her. Many of the same customers came back over and over; she was their private dancer and each man believed she was secretly attracted to him. But it was just a job that paid well. A little reefer before going on stage was all she needed to get her moves going.

Marge, the 65-year old club owner, told her about the oil boom in North Dakota and the big money being thrown around.

Girls were make $3000 a week if they could get into the gentleman's club—but you had to pass an audition.

Marge wasn't sure if that meant sex with the club owner in the back room or an audition on the pole.

"*Carpe Diem*," Marge told her. "That means seize the day, honey. Don't wait for life to come to you."

Lisa checked Google for dancing jobs in Williston and found the Queen of Hearts club was hiring. She had no possessions, nor pets, so packing was an afternoon job. If she was going to make the move, she had to get there before winter – and it was already October. She told

Marge goodbye – she was heading out of town.

Traveling at night was her thing. You couldn't see what was behind you, or what was ahead of you. When the sun came up, you were in a new world, free of your past. She wasn't running from anything; she was suffering from a "failure to launch."

If she could pay off her $90,000 in student loans, and make another $50,000, she could move anywhere and start over. That was the plan. She needed $140,000 from Williston.

~~~

Jerry Ebson walked to a taxi outside the Williston airport. He was grateful to stretch his legs after the long flight from Pennsylvania to North Dakota. His lanky six-foot-four frame had been scrunched in a dirty airplane seat for hours.

The cabbie dumped his two bags in the trunk and they pulled away.

"Where ya headed guy?" asked the cabbie.

"The Williston Daily building," Ebson replied.

"Ha, well it ain't really a building, so to speak, it's a storefront. Are you a new reporter?" asked the cabbie.

"Yes I am."

"You'll like working there. Ditzy is a good gal, she's done a lot of good things for the community. And it's busier than hell around here. You'll have a lot to do."
~~~

"Who's Ditzy?" asked Jerry.

"Ditzy is the publisher. She inherited the paper from her old man. That's not her real name of course, but that's what everyone calls her....except you of course," he laughed.

"She's making a ton of money now. Before the oil boom she was barely making it. But now, look around; this place is swarming with people, new business and all that easy oil money. She's making a bucket-load of money now," said the cabbie.

The cab pulled up to a brick storefront with a glass window stenciled in gold leaf:

Williston Daily

He paid the cabbie, grabbed his bags and walked inside. A pudgy receptionist looked up from her messy desk, saw the baggage and smiled.

"You're the new guy," she said. "My name is Gloria; I'm the intake person here. All the phone calls and walk-ins are my problem. You get to work on the fun stuff."

"I'm Jerry Ebson," he held out his hand.

"Any relation to Buddy?" she asked.

"Buddy?" he looked puzzled.

"Never mind, you're too young to remember Jed Clampett," Gloria said.

"So Ditzy is gone now, but she'll be back sometime in the afternoon. She rides her horses every day. We don't see her in the office much."

"You call her Ditzy too?" asked Jerry.

"Well not to her face, of course, but she wouldn't care. Everyone calls her that," said Gloria.

"Think I'd be safe calling her Miss Gloe?" asked Jerry.

"Yeah sure. That's fine," she said. "Just don't ask her about horses. She's a horse-nut. Now that she's flush with cash, she's buying horses left and right. It's all she cares about or talks about."

"Now about your lodging. The *Daily* owns a house just down the street. There's a room for you there. It's impossible to get a hotel room or rent a room in Williston. So this house is like a boarding house that Ditzy rents out to white collar types. She can't let the oil workers use it because they're such slobs. You get the room for free, but you will eventually share the house with a few other people," she said. "Hope you don't mind."

She opened a desk drawer, rummaged around and pulled out keys hanging from a round red-n-white fishing bobber.

"Here's the key to the front door and another for your room, which is upstairs, it's the blue room. There's a pink room also but that's for women," she said as she handed him the key.

"I'd take you there but I'm the only one here right now. Just go down the street one block. When you see a two-story house with a front porch that's painted green, that's it," she stated. "Tomorrow, after you're settled in, we'll get your computer logged in and you can start. We have two company cars, so you can take one out and get familiar with the area," she said.

"Sounds good. Thanks for your help. See you tomorrow," said Jerry and he turned and walked out the door.

~~~

Marty Fitzgerald glanced around the City Council chambers as the towns-people ambled into the room. As Mayor of Williston, he could vote on issues and manipulate the agenda of the Council. When he was elected, civic-governance was something that interested him; managing the city in a proactive way, rather than by crisis. *An eye to the future* was his campaign slogan.

After the oil companies arrived in Williston, his agenda changed; it was time to *make money.* Get rich, sell everything and move to Las Vegas. Get away from the nasty Dakota weather. Go somewhere he could golf every day, and fuck a young whore from time to time. At age 63, there wasn't much life remaining and he was tired of pissing it away for nothing.

He owned a small hardware store in town that was doing quite well since the oil men showed up. Tools and equipment were flying off the shelves. But the money wasn't coming in fast enough. He knew how to read people and play to their needs, their emotions; his plan was to fleece the oil men for everything he could take. But he needed the other councilmen to see things *his way.*

Fitzgerald rose to his feet and banged the gavel twice
~~~

before speaking.

"All rise as we commence the invocation by Reverend Johnson."

The audience rose to their feet and the men took off their hats. Reverend Johnson, a spindly man in his 50's with a gray goatee that made him look more like Leon Trotsky than a preacher, trudged to the front of the room, a bit too slowly in Fitzgerald's opinion, slightly taxing his patience. The preacher recited a mundane bible passage. The people were seated.

"I now call this meeting to order," Fitzgerald said calmly. "Do we have any new motions today before we begin our discussion of the planning and zoning variances?"

A hand shot up from Councilman Steve Gaylor.

"I make a motion that we abolish the religious invocation at the beginning of these meetings, as it clearly is a violation of the Separation Clause that prohibits church and state co-mingling at governmental functions," stated Gaylor.

A murmur went through the audience, heads turned as the *shock and awe* of his proposal found unwilling hearts and minds.

"Mr. Gaylor," said Fitzgerald, "we've been having an invocation at these meetings as long as I can remember. Why the opposition to a few religious words at the start of the meeting."

"Besides it being unconstitutional, it's very

exclusionary to always have this invocation by a Christian minister. There may be Jews, Muslims, Atheists, or other faiths present in the room that do not want to bow their heads to words of a different religious doctrine than their own. We could experiment by having a different religious invocation each meeting," stated Gaylor in a calm voice.

"Well I'm not going to listen to any invocation by a Muslim, I can tell you that," snorted Fitzgerald.

"I understand your unwillingness to show respect for a religion other than your own. Thus the reason why we should abolish these invocations," Gaylor stated.

The room was silent. The Reverend sat bug-eyed, his mouth hanging open. Fitzgerald looked around the room.

The logic made sense, but a tradition was a tradition; it didn't seem right to take that away or alter it for some damn Muslim or Jew. Everything else in town was changing; maybe this was good timing to get rid of it.

He didn't give a shit about religion anyway; he was there to make money. But he needed to pretend that the issue mattered, because the audience was filled with townspeople who were very religious, some of them were actually devout.

"Mr. Gaylor, I propose that we table this discussion until our next meeting, at which time we can put it on the agenda and open the floor for public comments," Fitzgerald said.

"Do I have a second for the motion?" he asked.

A hand shot up from a scowling council member and

that was the end of it.

"Now that we've put that issue to rest, let us begin our regular meeting tonight. We have several important variances on the agenda that we need to take into consideration," Fitzgerald said.

"The first item is a change in zoning from agricultural to industrial for Lind Implement Company," he continued.

This was a sweet-heart deal for him, and he anticipated no problems ramming it through. Fitzgerald had already worked out a deal with Leroy Lind. Fitzgerald would move his hardware store inside Lind's new twenty-thousand foot store. Lind agreed to give him the space for free if he could push the variance through, so this was win-win for both of them. He just needed to keep the deal secret until after the building was completed, when Lind would announce their "new partnership" to the community.

"Do we have any comments or discussion on this variance?" Fitzgerald asked the council.

There was no discussion because the councilmen had already agreed upon the variance at a private meeting at the Family Kitchen restaurant. That's how most of the agreements were made; outside of the council chambers. When they were in-session they had to pretend they were cogitating over the issues. They would talk at length about the issue; how a decision might impact the community. Behind the scenes, *the fix was in.*

"All in favor,"

All the hands went up.

"Those opposed."

No hands went up.

"The motion has passed."

Fitzgerald looked to the audience and gave a slight nod of his head to Lind, as he got up from his seat. *They would meet for drinks at the Old Saloon in a few hours.*

"The next order of business is consideration of a variance for Baker-Stewart Oil Company for a chemical storage warehouse, acid plant with mud blending, explosive storage bunker, and radioactive storage bunker," Fitzgerald said, squinting his eyebrows hard. He wanted to give the impression to the viewing audience that this variance was a *cause for concern and wouldn't likely go through.*

Fitzgerald wanted it to go through, he just needed to work out a "suitcase deal" with the Baker-Stewart people first. He liked getting suitcases from these oil-rich Texans. They were sleazy, corrupt, church-attending bastards. They were also results-oriented people who delivered cash. The right kind of *quid pro quo.*

The Baker-Stewart variance hadn't been "worked out" yet. He couldn't assure the Texans that he could ameliorate the fears of the other council members. Several councilmen were very concerned about acid, dynamite and radioactive materials being stored on the edge of town.

$100,000 for this, minimum. Too big for a suitcase, he'd ask them for gold bars.

"The floor is open for discussion," Fitzgerald said.

He looked into the crowd and saw the two Baker-Stewart "fixers" in the audience. They were watching closely, ready to report to corporate how much cash it was going to take to get the deal done. The fixers were a couple notches down the corporate ladder from real lobbyists; real lobbyists bought votes in state assemblies and the federal government. These guys made things happen on a local level.

After an hour of discussion, too many questions and concerns had been raised. Fitzgerald made a motion to table the variance to the next session and the council members stood up to go home. Fitzgerald's phone had a message from the Baker-Stewart men.

Rendezvous on the edge of town. Highway 2

Sliding into his Lexus, he turned on the headlights and drove west, towards the edge of town. He ran his hand over the leather seats. He smiled when he thought about how he got the car for free from Kodiak Resources. They had kindly given him the car when he pushed through a variance to build a 300-bed man camp. Now he was going to launch another sweet deal - this time he wanted six-figure retirement money.

The Baker-Stewart men were standing outside their rental car. Fitzgerald was in no hurry, he wanted to show restraint and control; he slowly exited the Lexus and sauntered over to the Texans.

The stumpy Texan, Rick Samuels, was clearly agitated.

"This is not going well. You promised us you could push this through. We have a timeline to keep and by the looks of things, progress has yet to be made," Samuels exploded.

"Stay calm Tex, this will all work out. I'm sure I can get you boys what you're after. The problem, as you could see for yourself, is that there are several additional council members that will require suitcases if you want this variance to go through," Fitzgerald said matter of fact.

"That won't be a problem," said Ralph, the other Texan.

"Yeah, well that's good," said Fitzgerald. "One thing I'm going to have to say up front, is that I have to carry more risk on this deal. I can't carry the day myself, so I'll have to work the other council members – which means I'm going to need more compensation than usual."

"What do you have in mind?" asked Ralph as he took a long drag on his cigarette.

"You've heard of a golden parachute? The huge bonus money lump-sums that are given to CEO's to walk-away? Well I'm going to need a golden suitcase. I've checked online and they sell something called a gold kilo-bar, which is thirty-two ounces. I want three of those," Fitzgerald smiled.

"Too much cash is hard to store; but I can easily store gold bars in my safe deposit box at the bank. It's for my retirement, so I won't be tempted to spend it," he chuckled.

The Texans didn't say anything. They were all business: smug, humorless-assholes.

Finally Ralph asked, "How many suitcases for the other councilmen."

"Well, I'm going to need three votes to go with mine; that would be four against three. So I think you should plan on three suitcases if you want this approved post-haste," Fitzgerald stated, trying to appear intellectual.

Ralph wrote notes on a flip pad.

"Okay, we'll get back to you this week," said Ralph.

"Start working your people," Samuels spat out.

"Your tone of voice is downright unfriendly Mr. Samuels," Fitzgerald said. "I thought we were on the same team here, you know, working together for a common cause."

"Matter of fact, I checked Baker-Stewart's capitalization and found that your company makes a gross profit of three billion dollars per year. That's a lot of money."

"Yeah," said Samuels.

"Well stop acting like I'm taking money from your grandmother's cookie jar! You guys have deep pockets," Fitzgerald laughed out loud.

The Texans got in their car and drove away. Fitzgerald pulled out his one-hitter, packed it tight, took a long toke, and stared up and the ink-black night sky.

~~~

Jerry Ebson awoke to the sounds of a car alarm squealing. For a small town, Williston had a hell-of-a-lot of noise, day and night. He threw on some jeans and shirt
~~~

and headed out the door looking to scout the town for breakfast. He found a diner and slipped inside. The place was packed with truck drivers and rough-looking tattooed men smoking cigarettes. A line formed up; people waiting to be seated. Jerry didn't want to stick around for that, so he bought a sweet roll and a cup of coffee to go for $12 dollars.

He strolled along the street, marveled with disdain as semi-truck after semi-truck rolled into town, Jake-braking the entire way. The sleepy little town had been corrupted by the lust for oil and all the riches the black syrup brought to those who extracted it. There was no stopping it.

He noticed the Alphabet Depot store had a "going out of business" sign in the window. He finished his roll and walked inside to see what remained. The store was messy. Some shelves were empty, others were jack-full of clutter and merchandise, mainly puzzles and books, posters and crayons. A fiftyish woman looked up from a display she was taking down and spoke,

"Can I help you find anything? We're closing down so things are in a bit of chaos right now."

"No, I'm new in town and just having a look around," Jerry said.

"Are you an oil worker?" she asked, with a fake smile on her face.

"No, I'm a reporter for the *Daily*," Jerry stated. "Why are you closing?"

"The owner increased my rent," she sighed. "I've been

here nine years, supplying school teachers and children with supplies. I suppose if I sold oil well parts or drill bits I would be okay, but selling low margin books to children doesn't leave enough money to pay $3,000 dollars per month rent."

"$3,000 thousand? Jerry exclaimed. "For this…maybe 1200 feet of space?"

"Yes, for past nine years my rent has been $650," she said.

"Wow, that's crazy. Can you find another retail space in town?" Jerry asked.

"No, this is the end of the line. All the rents have gone up. Where did you find a place to live? There's nothing available," she asked.

"The *Daily* has a house in town; I'm staying in one of the rooms," he said.

"Oh that's right; I forgot that Ditzy owned that house. You're very lucky. But on the other hand, if she didn't give you the room for free, she wouldn't have any reporters because you couldn't afford rent in this town on a newspaper salary," she stated bluntly, a bit angered by his sweet-deal.

"It is what it is, I guess," Jerry responded as he backed up to the door. "Good luck," he said as he walked out the door.

~~~

The front door to the *Daily* was already open when
~~~

Jerry arrived at 7:45 a.m. Jerry had been up since 6:00 a.m., so it pleased him the door was open early.

Start the day, getting it going, get things done.

"Good morning Jerry," Gloria yelled out from the back of the building. She sauntered up to his desk. "There's coffee brewing in the break room, help yourself."

"So where's the municipal court in town? City hall right?" Jerry asked.

"You got it. It's a block over, same building as the cop-shop," she replied. "Are you going to attend civil court today?"

"Yeah, just the morning cases, then I'll be back to write 'em up," Jerry stated.

"Well, have fun. You get to hear citations against oil workers caught pissing in the Walmart parking lot or the alley behind the Queen of Hearts strip club," she said.

Jerry found the non-descript police station. The court room was off to one side. He took a seat near the front so he could hear the proceedings. There were quite a few dirty-looking oil workers sitting in chairs, awaiting their cases.

The judge entered the room and everyone rose to attention. The first few cases were traffic citations for speeding and blowing through stop signs followed by disorderly conduct cases for public urination and fisticuffs; none of which merited a story. Finally, something interesting occurred.

The District Attorney, a short, dumpy forty-five year old man with nasty "pizza face" acne scars, read the citation to the court.

"On October 9, defendant Steve Ervin used an extension cord to plug in a heater for his 1997 Chevy Astro van at the Raymond Family Community Center. The Community Center is publicly owned; therefore Mr. Ervin is stealing from the taxpayers. I recommend the maximum punishment of thirty days in jail and a thousand dollar fine."

The Judge looked at a document in his hands and lifted his eyes to the defendant.

"How do you plead Mr. Ervin?" asked the judge.

"No contest," stated Ervin.

"Very well, let's hear your side of the story, Mr. Ervin," the judge said in a calm voice.

"Your honor, I moved here five weeks ago and I live out of my van because there is no housing available. I'm a night stocker at Walmart so I'm gainfully employed in the community. I'm also a member of the Community Center and use the facility daily. I was totally unaware that it was against the law to use the electrical outlet to run my space heater for an hour; especially since I'm a member.

There are other businesses in town that allow people to use their outlets. The Community Center has no signs prohibiting this usage. I have never had a ticket of any kind my entire life. Not even a parking ticket. If I am convicted of this, I will lose my job. Walmart will fire me if I have to serve jail time. So I ask the court to dismiss the charges against me," Ervin stated with pleading eyes.

The D.A. looked at the judge, "I'd like police officer Lieutenant Janson to speak on the issue."

A cop in his late twenties, big build with a blond flat-top hair approached the bench.

"Williston police don't go looking for people who are illegally plugged-in to private electrical outlets, but if we get a complaint, we react to it. In this case we did receive a complaint. Stealing is stealing; I don't care if it's ten cents worth of electricity. He's still stealing it," Janson said.

Ervin shook his head. "I admit to using the electricity, but the fact remains that if I am convicted, this will be on my permanent record. I'll have to disclose this on every job application for the rest of my life. Ruining my life for this – it's just not right. This will be on my record forever," Ervin moaned.

The Judge nodded his headed. "You may all take your seats."

He picked up a pen and jotted something down. "Mr. Ervin I'm going to sentence you to two days in jail for this violation," he said flatly. "Please call the next case."

Ervin stood up and stormed from the room. Jerry quietly slipped out after him and approached him as he was lighting up a cigarette outside the building.

"You got a raw deal in there," Jerry stated.

"Fucking kangaroo court. They just fucking railroaded me. My job's gone now," Ervin said.

"Maybe you could schedule the days off with Walmart and arrange it with the court for to serve time on your days off," Jerry suggested.

Ervin nodded his head. "Yeah, maybe. That's a good idea. I'll see what the HR people say at Wally-world."

"Are you a reporter?" asked Ervin.

Jerry nodded.

"Make sure you write this up. People should know how we are treated here. We're treated like fucking stray dogs or something. We're just trying to get our lives going again. People come here needing a new start, for whatever reason. It's hard enough living out of car or a trailer; city has no reason to be so punitive with something as petty as this. Pisses me off, I tell you. Enough to make me and probably others, strike back somehow. Don't print that!" he stated.

"You know what I mean?" he asked. "You can't fuck people over like this; pretty soon the other shoe will drop. They'll see. I'm not the vindictive type; just want to be left alone to do my own thing. But there are other guys; you go down to Walmart and talk to 'em in the parking lot. You'll meet a lot of crazies over there. Some of those guys will get back at these small town fucks."

"What's at the Walmart parking lot?" asked Jerry.

"You ain't been over there yet? Christ, the place is an RV lot of squatters. It's like a shantytown on wheels. You better go take a look," said Ervin. "You're newer than me, ain't ya?"

"Yes, I just arrived," said Jerry. "Learning as I go. Thanks for the tip on Walmart; I'll go scout that out," Jerry said.

As they were talking, Mark Janson, the Williston cop locals called "Marky-Mark" on account of his resemblance to actor Mark Walberg, came out of the building. He lit up a cigarette and eyed down the two men. Ervin got nervous and walked away. Janson ambled up to Jerry.

"Are you writing for the *Daily*?" he asked.

"Yes I am," Jerry replied, holding out his hand for a shake. "Jerry Ebson."

They shook hands and the cop snuffed out his cigarette on the sidewalk.

"How would you like to go for a drive around town with me in the squad car. It'll give you some perspective on the challenges we face here?" the cop asked.

"Yeah, sure. Let's go. I have nothing going on today other than to write up this electricity stealing case," Jerry replied.

They walked to his squad car and drove onto the busy main drag.

"Do you think you could show me the Walmart parking lot?" asked Jerry.

"Oh sure, I drive through there several times a day. It's a real hot-spot for us," replied the cop.

They drove a few blocks and the Walmart signed loomed in the distance. As they pulled in the parking lot

Jerry's mouth fell open.

"Holy Christ," said Jerry. "Looks like the aftermath of hurricane Katrina."

The lot was jammed with RV's and trailers. End to end, side by side; wherever they could squeeze together on the outside perimeter of the lot. Little shanty-towns inter-connected with blue tarps had come into existence. Most of the RV's never moved locations.

"This place is a hot-bed of illegal activity. These guys are pissing in the lot, selling and using drugs, moving guns, running whores. Right under lights of this billion-dollar corporation. The locals don't like to shop here, especially at night. The women get harassed so they won't even come here. You get a bunch of horny men all bunched together with jugs of liquor and meth going around, anything can happen. So we have a strong presence out here," Janson stated.

"There's the electricity guy over there," said Jerry.

They could see Ervin surrounded by a few men, telling his story, waving his hands in the air.

"He's riling up the crowd," said the cop. "Most of these guys here are fuck-heads, just like him. They have no skills. They're out of options in life, so they leave wherever they were and come up here in hopes of making big-bucks. But they won't make big-bucks because they are unskilled or their chemical issues prevent them from being hired," said Janson.

"Most of the oil companies and trucking companies demand a drug test before they hire. These guys have all failed it. I know they've failed because they'd be working otherwise. They'd be out on the job or living at a man-camp," he continued. "So we keep a close eye on these idiots.

The cop looked at Jerry.

"What do you think?" he asked.

"Well, it's certainly a mess. How long is Walmart gonna let it stay like this? Jerry asked.

"We don't know for sure, but I do know their management is getting tired of the situation. I think any day now they will roust these deadbeats from their parking lot. That would be contrary to their corporate policy, but I think they'll do it on the down-low so the public at large doesn't hear about it," Janson stated.

"Then what?" Jerry asked? "Where will these guys go?"

"Don't know. They can't park their trailers within the city of Williston. We have an ordinance against that. So they'll have to go rural, or find a private area, or go home. Not our problem," he said smirking. "But, it'll be harder to keep tabs on these jackasses."

~~~

Lisa Wagner arrived at the outskirts of Williston, only to find herself stuck in a traffic jam. A line of semi-trucks as far as she could see stretched out ahead of her.

A fucking traffic jam in North Dakota? What the fuck!
~~~

Slowly traffic crept forward until she was able to take a side street and get into the town. She stopped at a few motels; they were all full. Clerks shaking their heads, telling her there were *no rooms available, anywhere.* This was unexpected. She'd never seen a town with no rooms available. But this was Williston.

She zigzagged around the residential areas hoping to see a sign for a room to rent or some type of lodging—but there was nothing. Just cars and trailers parked in yards. She was tired, hungry, and frazzled, and beginning to think she had made a huge mistake.

She spotted the newspaper office and decided to buy a newspaper, take a look at the classifieds.

Maybe there were rooms for rent.

She parked out front and went inside.

Jerry heard the "dingle-bell" above the door and looked up. He did a double-take as the gorgeous young woman entered the office area and approached the counter. Gloria was away so he got up from his desk to have a closer look and see if he could help her. She was the clearly the most beautiful thing in Williston.

"Hi, can I help you with something?" he asked.

"I'd like to buy a paper. Something with classified ads. I just drove into town and I need a room for a few days," she said.

"Here's a copy of yesterday's paper. The ads are in the back," he said, handing her the paper. "There's no charge for yesterday's news," he laughed.

She smiled and looked around the office for a chair. "Would it be okay if sat in your lobby and read the ads?" she asked.

"Go right ahead. I'll be at my desk if you need anything else. Where are you from?" Jerry asked.

"Denver," she replied as she turned and sat in the chair. He noticed how worried she looked.

After a few minutes she put the paper down and starred out into the room.

"Excuse me," she called to Jerry. "I don't see any rooms or lodging available in the paper. Do you know of anywhere that I can get a room for tonight?"

"Well, no, sorry. I just arrived in town a couple of days ago, so I don't really know anyone," Jerry replied.

"Are you here for a job? Maybe your employer has some options for you," he suggested.

"No, I don't have a job yet," she replied, tears running down her face.

Jerry was getting a bit rattled by the show of emotion; she was imploding.

"Hey, I have an idea, just a temporary thing. The house I live in has an extra room. Nobody is in it right now. Would you be okay staying in a private house?" he asked.

"Really? Yes, that we would be wonderful," she smiled. "I don't want to sleep in my car, so even a couch would be okay with me."

"My name is Jerry, I'm a reporter here," he stuck out his hand to shake.

"Lisa Wagner," she shook his hand.

"Give me a minute to shut down my computer and I'll show you where the house is."

Jerry logged off the pc, grabbed his jacket and walked out the front door with Lisa following a few steps behind.

"Are you parked out here?" he asked.

"Yes, I have the red VW -- hop in," she said.

Jerry noticed the passenger seat was filled with snacks, a water bottle, cell phone charger and make-up bottles. She cleared the seat and they pulled away. He directed her to the house and they parked out front on the street.

"Do you want to see the room first before you make up your mind? Jerry asked.

"No way. Beggars can't be choosers and right now I'm a beggar," she said as she popped her trunk. She pulled out a large suitcase with airport wheels and set it beside the curb.

"Let me grab your bag for you," Jerry said, as he picked up the heavy suitcase.

He led her into the old, plain-Jane house. She looked around at the living room and the mundane kitchen. "It's nice. Reminds me of my grandma's house in Ottumwa."

"Are you from Iowa?" Jerry asked.

"You know where that is? Ottumwa? Most people have no clue," she said.

"I was born and raised there. I moved to Colorado after high school to attend college. I had to get out of Iowa," she stated.

"Let me show you the room," Jerry said, as he walked up the narrow staircase with her luggage in hand.

"I'm in the blue room," he said as they walked past his room, "and you're in the pink room," he said.

Her face lit up as she entered the room. "This is the same color I had in my room when I was a little girl," she said. "I love it."

"How long can I stay here?" Lisa asked.

"I have no clue. I'm not sure you *can* stay here. It's not my house. It's owned by the newspaper and right now no one is in the room," Jerry responded.

"I can ask tomorrow. Maybe they'll rent it to you by the week or month. I just don't know. For tonight, it's a better place to crash than sleeping in your car."

"Thank you so much," Lisa said, "you didn't have to do this. I will buy you dinner for helping me out."

"Not likely. The restaurants in this town are packed, around the clock. Unless you want to wait for fifty minutes," Jerry said.

"Why don't you get settled. I have to go back to the office to finish a story, then we can walk the main drag and see if we can get some dinner," Jerry suggested. "See you at five."

~~~

After putting the finishing touches on the "stolen electricity" story, Jerry e-mailed it to the editor for the next day's edition. The production staff laid out the paper during the afternoons and printed at night for distribution the next day. The place was a frenzy of people as they scrambled to get all the photos and articles into the software.

Jerry wanted to ask Gloria about using the extra room, but she wasn't around.

To hell with it. They're too busy to care anyway.

He walked back to the house and found Lisa waiting in the living room, reading an *Architecture Digest* magazine.

"Ready to eat?" he asked her.

"Ready Freddy," she replied.

He liked her casualness; her friendly demeanor didn't go hand-in-hand with his life experiences with knockout-blonds. Usually they were aloof, bitchy, and self-centered. On the other hand, he had something *she needed*, so she was highly motivated to be 'nice.'

As they walked along the street, men in passing cars and trucks yelled out catcalls and obscenities; hot-looking women were rare in Williston. Lisa attracted attention wherever she went – indoor or outdoor. The first restaurant had an hour wait; the next one had a line of people waiting outside the door. They were both
~~~

famished and feeling a bit stressed.

"How about we hit the grocery store and I'll cook for you?" Jerry asked.

"How about we team cook," she replied.

The grocery store had everything they wanted; a big piece of fresh salmon, some bread, butter, carrots, even some fresh dill. They grabbed a bottle of white wine and they each contributed a twenty-dollar bill when the cashier rang it up.

"Does this qualify as a first-date?" Jerry asked, have joking.

"I think it does. I've never had a date like this," Lisa laughed.

~~~

Lisa awoke in the pink room to the sound of a semi-truck blasting its horn. The long drive had made her tired beyond anticipation. But the peaceful room had been a god-send, except she didn't believe in gods. She was spiritual in a different way. The Universe was awake and listening; all you had to do was ask for it – *call it in.*

Now she needed to find abundance. She had made it to Williston; time to make some money. She found the bathroom and the crude shower spigot hooked to a hose. She showered and took time with her hair. The house was quiet; Jerry was already at work. She put on her make-up and some stretch leggings with a loose-fitting fishnet top over a sports-bra.
~~~

Dress for audition. Gotta look hot!

The Queen of Hearts strip club was easy to find. It had a façade of flat rock inlay with gaudy-green boards running vertically up the wall. She shuddered at the horrible design.

Designed by an idiot.

Her first thought was that the façade should have been red with playing card "hearts" stenciled on the vertical boards.

She parked on the street and went inside. It was dark, smelly, but the music was good. At least they had a jukebox with some decent tunes. She asked the bartender, a fat slob with a cigarette in his hand, if she could talk to the manager.

"Hang on a sec, cutie. I'll give her a shout," he said with a leering grin.

She analyzed the club. There are gentlemen's clubs and there are strip clubs – the differences are huge. A gentlemen's club has champagne VIP rooms to up-sell the clients; a strip club has a jukebox, metal folding chairs, and a dirty one-hole bathroom. This pit was a strip club – nasty smelling black carpet, cheesy pink neon lights, and a dinky stage in a corner with a disco mirror ball hanging from the ceiling and mirrors around the single-pole stage.

The slob bartender picked up a house phone and talked. He hung up the phone and pointed to a side door.

"Go through that door. Brandy is waiting for you," he

said, as he went back to his cigarette.

Lisa flung her hair back and strutted to the door, as the patrons turned their heads to follow her every move. A bouncer opened the door with the PRIVATE – EMPLOYEES ONLY sign and she pushed through. She walked down a narrow hall, past changing rooms until she found the manager's office. Brandy was a red-head in her forties.

"Hello Darling, come inside," she said with a European accent.

Lisa introduced herself and gave a brief overview of her experience.

"So you've been dancing in Denver then; that is good. You have experience," Brandy said. "We have some European girls here; some girls from Los Angeles and some from New Orleans. They come and go by airplane."

"I'm planning on living here; I want to work every day," Lisa said.

"Every day?" Brandy said with surprise. "You must have some very large bills to pay. Did you find a place to stay? Housing is not easy to come by. Many of the girls that work here stay right here at the club; we have bunks for them."

"Yes, I have a friend in town that I'm staying with," Lisa lied.

"Lucky you. Unless you have a camper there is nowhere to stay in Williston."

"My rules are very simple; no drug use in the building, no prostitution while you are working, and be on-time for your shift. We have men coming in here at all hours, six days a week, we are closed on Sundays because the city shuts down to worship Jesus. You must cover your nipples. Lap dances are twenty-dollars, and the tip-out rate for the bartender and waitress is twenty-five percent.

"The typical girl makes $2,000 per week. You may do better than that. Every girl is an independent contractor – so you receive 1099 on the earnings we pay you. Your tips are yours to report or not report, we don't care," she stated. "Fuck the IRS, right?"

"When would you like to start?" Brandy asked.

"Tomorrow would be fine. What shifts are available?" Lisa asked.

"That will work; we have open shifts every day. We will look at the schedule. Once you are here for a while, you will get seniority and you can pick your shifts. Not like a union shop or anything, it's a revolving door of dancers here, so if you stay for more than a couple months, you'll be able to pick your shifts. The weekends are the best; the men get paid on Friday's and spend their money on the weekends," Brandy said.

"I'll be here tomorrow and every day after that," Lisa said smiling.

"You are a very determined girl," Brandy said, "I like that in people."

~~~
~~~

"I gotta piss," Larry groaned, as he awoke in the back seat of the Blazer. "My eyeballs are floating; stop on the shoulder so I can whip my dick out."

"Yeah me too," Wayne said.

Wayne slowly angled the Blazer and camper off the freeway, onto the shoulder. They got out and walked to the ditch.

"Time to drain the main vein," Larry laughed. "I could use some chow. How far are we from Williston?" he asked.

"About another thirty minutes," Wayne stated. "We'll be parking the can-of-ham in Walmart anyway, so let's get food inside the store and save some money.

"What about coffee? I need a hot cup of Joe. My head is pounding and I need to take a shit," Larry complained.

"If we see a garbage food place near an exit I'll pull in. You can get all your needs met at a McDonalds," Wayne laughed.

Wayne didn't eat that fast-food shit; but Larry did. Corporate food was made for maximum profiteering, not nutrition or health. The corporate fucks didn't care about clogged veins, or obesity, or trans-fat bloated, jelly-belly people. They wanted their stock price to go up, so they could exercise their options and sell tens of thousands of shares. That's how the game was rigged. Who could blame them? That was their job; maximize profits regardless of the human consequences. The mantra repeated over and over by every corporation in America.

Wayne couldn't find a freeway McDonald's so they drove straight into Williston and pulled into the Walmart parking lot.

"Holy Fuck," Wayne yelled.

The place was packed with trailers. Finding even a small spot for the can-of-ham was going to present a problem.

"There's a Walmart guy there," Larry said, pointing his finger at a man wearing a blue associate vest. "He's waving us over."

Wayne rolled down his window to talk to the guy, a gray-beard, fifty-year-old who looked like Redford's *Jeremiah Johnson.*

"Welcome to Williston, we're just about full at the inn, but there are a couple spots you can get into. What year is your "canned ham" trailer? I haven't seen one of these in a while," the Associate asked.

Wayne ignored the small talk. "So where's the spot I can park this? We're both hungry and tired, and he needs to take a shit," pointing his thumb at Larry.

"Just pull up next to that big-fucking Winnebago and back it in. I'll tell the guy he has to move his lawn chairs and grill to the other side," the Associate said. "You might want to bring your own ass-wipe into the shitter; some of the stalls are out and I'd hate to see you spray the bowl and not have any paper. Know what I mean?" the guy laughed.

"Thanks for the tip," Larry yelled out. "I'll bring my

own skid."

Wayne parked the trailer next to the other RV's and they went inside.

"Look at this fucking place," Wayne barked, shaking his head, "It's like a god-damn zoo or a carnival. We need to get oil jobs with a man-camp and get the fuck out of here."

PRIVATE PROPERTY
NO CAMPING
THANK YOU
WAL★

CHAPTER II

"For the love of Christ, who would do such a thing?" yelled Gloria into the phone. Jerry had just walked in the front door of the *Daily*.

"Hold on a sec," Gloria said into the phone, "Hey Jerry, before you get going on anything, grab a digital camera and head down to Main Street. The police called and somebody vandalized all the stores downtown. Marky-Mark is down there now writing up a report," she said.

Jerry took a Ford Focus fleet vehicle, and drove around town until he saw the squad car in front of the JC Penney store.

"Good morning Mark," he said to the big, small-town cop.

"Hi Jerry. You brought your camera today," Mark said.

"So what's the story with the busted glass?" Jerry asked as he framed up a shot with the camera.

"All along this side of the street. Some oil-can-Harry busted the windows last night. Must have use a heavy steel pin and hit 'em just hard enough to fracture the glass, but not bust the window out."

Jerry glanced up the street at the store fronts with shattered glass. "Somebody's mad at the town for something," he said.

He looked up at Marky-Mark, "Probably one-too-many speeding tickets Mark."

"I never tire of writing citations for out-of-state assholes," Mark joked, not really joking.

"I suppose each of these broken windows will fall below the deductible for the store owners. So their insurance won't cover it; they'll have to pay out-of-pocket," Jerry surmised.

"You'd make a good cop," Marky-Mark grinned.

Jerry ignored the comment.

"So how do you know it was an oil-worker that did this?" Jerry asked.

"I don't. But a rose, is a rose, is a rose," Mark sang out.

"I thought you were gonna say if it looks like a duck, quacks like a duck," Jerry countered. "That's how they used to find Communists during the Cold War."

"No, but I may use that one tomorrow, or later today," Mark shot back.

"Suppose it wasn't an oil guy that did this," Jerry asked.

"Well who else would it be? Mark asked. "Somebody is pissed off about something."

"Maybe not," Jerry offered, "what if it's about money?"

"Money?" Mark cocked his head askew.

"Yeah, you know. Motive, Means, Opportunity," Jerry recited.

"Okay, let me ask you this," said Jerry, "who in this community will profit or could profit by the destruction of these windows."

"Well, that would be Lou Harmon at Harmon glass, but he only does auto glass, or the Mayor, he sells this kind of glass at the hardware store," Mark said.

"Good idea, Jerry, I'll go interview the Mayor right away. I'll ask him if he was out here, busting windows last night; then I'll have him sign my paycheck while I'm in his office interrogating him."

Jerry walked along the street, taking pictures of the storefronts. Another story was shaping up.

~~~

"I have an appointment with Mayor," stated Derrick Chilton to the homely-looking secretary at city hall.

Jesus that woman is ugly.

"He's in his office, just knock on the door," she replied with no interest whatsoever.

Chilton knocked on the door and peeked in the room. The Mayor was working on a laptop computer.

"Come on in, have a chair," said Fitzgerald. "I'm just looking at some numbers on this Excel spreadsheet. You ever use Excel or any of the Microsoft products?" the Mayor asked.

"Only Word, and just for writing letters. I'm not a power user," replied Chilton.
~~~

"Well, those guys at Microsoft are the smartest, dumbest fuckers on the planet. They've been making this Office suite for twenty years, and each time they come out with a new version, I have to re-learn the user-interface all over again. They move things around. All the menus and shortcuts are different. Really stupid. Can you imagine buying a car and having to re-learn all the controls because Ford decided to move the gas pedal to the left foot?" Fitzgerald exclaimed.

"That's why Apple is doing so well," Fitzgerald continued. "Microsoft hires Ph.D. brainiacs from India. They're all extremely smart in a mathematical kind of way, but they couldn't design a birdhouse. It's clear to me, that Apple does the opposite. They hire 'divergent thinkers' for their teams so the brainiacs don't take control and make stupid decisions."

Chilton just nodded his head.

"Here's another one for you," the Mayor continued. "Do you ever use a jump-drive to move files around? If you right-click on a drive, a menu will pop up that gives you choices. Those idiots at Microsoft put the 'eject' choice, right next to the 'format' choice. How stupid can you be? People can accidently format their drives if they're not paying attention."

"Anyway, you didn't come here talk about Microsoft's shitty software. You came here to talk about getting a taxi license for your handicap van," Fitzgerald said, looking him in the eye.

"Could you do me a favor and shut that door so we can have some privacy?" asked the Mayor.

Chilton closed the door and took his seat.

"Now the City of Williston code of ordinances classifies a taxi as a seven person vehicle or less. You have converted a handicapped bus into a taxi vehicle for shuttling oil workers into the strip clubs and back. That's a clever idea. Unfortunately it runs contrary to the regulations so you're going to need a special permit – which I can arrange," Fitzgerald stated.

"I see you understand my situation," Chilton smiled. "What's the special permit going to cost me?"

Here comes the other shoe dropping.

"Oh this isn't much of big deal. It's not like you want to build a man-camp," Fitzgerald laughed. "I have to tell you, I love drinking scotch at night. Do you know how much a bottle of Cutty Sark is now? A 750-milliliter size is $25 dollars a bottle; I drink probably three bottles a week. That's a case per month."

"Maybe you should cut down?" Chilton laughed. "You could save a lot of money over the course of a year."

"Here's what I was thinking," Fitzgerald snickered. "I'm thinking that you could supply me a year's worth of Cutty Sark. I have plenty of room in my garage to stack up twelve cases. It would save me travel time to the liquor store. If I have a year's supply of scotch in my garage, I know I can get you the special permit to operate your strip club bus within city limits. If you don't have that permit, you can't legally drop people off at the strip clubs. The police would be waiting to ticket you. And that's not a parking ticket; that's a city ordinance violation and those citations are thousands of dollars. We need to work together to prevent that from happening. You know how overzealous these small town cops are. Just last week they sent a guy to jail for stealing electricity," Fitzgerald said.

"I can see your point," Chilton said. "I'm pretty good at reading tea leaves too," no longer smiling as he added up the dollar amount in his head.

"I may have to run to Dickenson to get that many cases. Will you be home tomorrow evening?" Chilton asked. "I can make the drop-off after dark."

"Splendid." Fitzgerald said smiling. He stood up and offered his hand to seal the deal.

"I will be home tomorrow night. In a couple of weeks, you should have your special use permit," Fitzgerald said.

Chilton walked out the door calculating the cost of the permit in his head.

Twelve bottles at $25 was $300 multiplied by 12 cases was $3600.

He would have to raid his E-trade account for the Mayor's scotch money.

~~~

Wayne rolled out of his bunk in the can-of-ham trailer and lit the propane stove for the coffee. He had prepped the coffee the night before so it was ready to go.

"I'm going in the store to brush my teeth and take a piss," he said to Larry who was still lying on a foam mattress.
~~~

"Watch the coffee in case it starts to boil over," Wayne said as he opened the door.

The toilets at the Walmart were a sight to behold – filthy, grimy, and stinking like a men's locker room. He made a mental note to use disinfectant wipes on his hands.

As he walked back to the trailer he noticed a large Winnebago with a "We're Hiring" banner on the side. He told Larry about it and poured a cup of coffee.

"I'm going to walk over there and ask them about jobs; be back in a few minutes," Wayne said.

He sauntered over to the employer trailer and stepped up the door and knocked. A man in his 30's opened the door.

"Come on in," said the guy.

"What we have available are various oil rig jobs. If you have a CDL you can haul water; if you have rig experience we can put you to work right away. Do you have either of those backgrounds?" the guy asked.

"Yes, we have CDL's, but we prefer to work on the drilling rigs, work long hours, whatever it takes," Wayne stated.

"There's more money to be made working the on the drill rigs, that's for sure, but it's harder work, longer hours, dirty, dangerous. If you're okay with that then the first step in the process is to pass a criminal background check and drug test. Once you're verified we can put your names on a list. The oil companies pull from that list to fill their ranks. Believe it or not, a lot of guys wash out.

Most can't get by the drug test, and the one's that do, a lot of them can't hack it for very long," the guy stated.

"Here are a few forms you need to fill out. Just social security, employment background, stuff like that. Now later today, there's a drug testing company that comes here every Monday. They have you piss in a bottle and they send it off for screening.

"How long does that take?" Wayne asked, "For the results to come back."

"Only a couple of days. They do the tox-screening at the Williston hospital lab," the guy said. "It takes a few days for the background check to come back."

"Okay thanks. We'll get these filled out and brought back," Wayne said.

"Oh, one more thing, there's a hundred dollar application fee for each person," the guy added as Wayne was getting up from his chair.

"That figures. Everyone's gotta make a buck out here," Wayne said flatly.

"Yeah, this RV don't run on thank you's," the guy said defensively.

~~~

Wayne showed Larry the papers and poured another coffee.

"I figured there would be a drug test," Larry said, "that sucks."
~~~

"Why?" asked Wayne.

"Well I smoke pot, and that stays in your blood for weeks," Larry said.

"I'm going to need some of your piss," Larry exclaimed.

"Yeah right."

"No I'm serious, I'm going to use your piss to get past the drug test," Larry said, as he was rummaging around in his duffel bag.

"How will you do that? They'll be looking at you while you piss," Wayne laughed.

"With this big guy," Larry said, pulling out a rubber-cock from his bag.

"What the fuck is that?" Wayne said.

"It's a Whizzinator. Haven't you seen these before?" The pro athletes been using these for years to defeat drug tests," Larry explained.

"You pour in good piss or synthetic piss, close the cap, then when you take your test, you have this in your pants. You pull it out and when you squeeze it, the good piss will come out the tip and into the plastic cup they give you," Larry instructed. "It's easy."

"You've done this before?" Wayne asked.

"Yes. They only test you when you get hired. After that they never test you again," Larry explained.

"They really make synthetic piss? You've got to be

kidding me," Wayne chuckled.

"Yes, they really make synthetic piss. Passing drug tests is big business," Larry said. "See, modern employers are like Nazis; they not only want your servitude, a good attitude, and love of company, they also want to control aspects of your *personal life.* Like your drug and alcohol intake. They say it's for safety and all that, but it's really about control. So, we gotta beat the man at his own game," Larry lectured. "Life's too short to not smoke pot."

That afternoon the drug testing bus pulled into the Walmart lot. Wayne noted the bus was actually a converted school bus with little plywood rooms for collecting the urine samples. Wayne went in first, Larry lagging behind a couple people so he could observe the intake process – and back out if necessary – just in case they threw a curveball he wasn't expecting.

He watched as Wayne handed his paperwork to the guy at the desk. Another guy handed him a small plastic bottle with a screw-on lid and directed him to one of the small outhouse doors. Wayne reemerged after a minute and gave Larry a smile.

Too easy. They didn't even watch.

When it was Larry's turn he took the vial into the room, used the Whizzinator and cruised out the door.

"Hey you," yelled the agent with the piss-vials.

Larry got suddenly scared and his face went red.

"Yes," he asked.

"You forgot to put the name sticker on your vial," the guy said, handing him his vial back.

Larry remembered the ID-sticker on his form. He removed the sticker and stuck it to the vial of piss. He hoped the guy wouldn't handle the vial, because the Whizzinator piss wasn't hot; it was room temperature.

The testing agent paid no attention to it. He put it in a rack. He was wearing rubber gloves anyway.

Wayne was waiting outside as Larry came out of the test van.

"Piece of cake," Larry said.

~~~

Two weeks later they were living in a man-camp outside of Williston. Wayne was sorry to sell the can-of-ham trailer, but he sold it for $2100, three-times the amount he had paid for it in St. Paul.

The man-camp was owned by Continental Oil. Three hundred men all packed together in a bunkhouse community. Not that anyone cared. They were all there to make money. The camp was a place to sleep and get some food; nothing else. Everyone was too tired for recreation.

The alarm clock buzzing woke Wayne and Larry from their deep sleep. Larry looked at the clock.

"Four a.m. Fuck!"

He rolled off his bed and put on his clothes. Wayne followed suit and they walked out the door, dressed in the
~~~

blue jumpsuits the company provided, with their yellow hardhats in hand. A bus took them to the rig and dropped them off, just as the sun was beginning to lift over the eastern horizon.

A stout oil worker in the same blue jumpsuit called the men to attention.

"My name is Gene and I'm the rig manger. That means I oversee all of you and also the operation of this rig. I know we have some new guys on the crew today. Safety is of utmost importance. While you are learning your jobs as roustabouts, keep your eyes open, listen, pay attention to what's going on, and ask questions. I will be instructing you as we go. But this is an on-going operation; not a training facility. What we used to call *on-the-job training*. Let's get going and conduct a safe operation," Gene finished.

The other men knew what to do and scattered out among the rig. Gene approached Wayne and Larry.

"Okay guys, I'm going to be working with you two today. I'm going to teach you the components of the rig, how it operates and how we get the oil out of the ground. We work seven days a week until we get this well going. There won't be much time for in-depth training. But I'll keep you up to speed as we move along," Gene said.

"The first thing I want to show you is the Kelly Spinner. That is the pneumatically driven spinner that is the heart of this rig. It spins the drill bit and the pipe up and down. It's operated by Tim, who is our Driller. He's in charge of the bits and controls the Spinner," Gene stated. "Be careful around this thing. If you get caught up in this it will spin you around like a rag doll."

"Your jobs are to use the tongs as we rig up and later rig down. The tongs allow us to connect the pipes that we drop into the shaft. This is dirty and dangerous work. So keep your eyes and ears open," he cautioned.

"Do either of you know anything about how we drill out here?" he asked.

Both men shook their heads, "no."

"The first step is the vertical shaft. We drill straight down, until we get past the water table, some sixty to a hundred feet. At that point we pull the bit out, insert another pipe sleeve and pour concrete into the pipe. That concrete flows out of the pipe and up the outside of the pipe sleeve and forms a tight barrier to isolate the water table from the drilling area. That way no contamination will occur," Gene said.

"After the concrete has set, we continue drilling down, way down, like a mile. That's a lot of pipe. Each pipe is thirty-feet long and weighs about five-hundred pounds. You guys will be putting that pipe into the ground by threading the pipes together, section after section, until we get to the kick-off point," Gene recited.

"The kick-off point is where we start to bend the drill angle from vertical to horizontal. Eventually, we will be drilling horizontal, which we call the Lateral."

"How the hell do you bend steel pipe?" Larry asked

"We don't bend it; the radius is so small the pipe slides right in," Gene answered.

"Once we have the Lateral completed, we perforate the adjacent rock formations with explosives. The shock from the explosives shatters the shale rock – which is where the oil is trapped. Then we pump high-pressure water into those cracks. The water is a mixture of sand from Wisconsin and some chemicals. They call this hydraulic fracturing. The high pressure water and sand bust up the shale in a big way, creating passages for the oil to flow out," Gene continued.

"We pump out the water and sand – after that it's all oil. We take the rig down, put a well-head on the casing and the oil flows until its depleted," he finished.

"Welcome to Williston boys!" yelled Gene.

~~~

They worked all day, every day, rain or shine from sunrise to sunset. Life on the drilling rig was work, eat, sleep – and getting yelled at.

Nobody talks on a rig – they shout. Who yells at whom, depends on the job. Roustabouts are on the bottom – they learn quickly – don't say the wrong thing to the wrong people, or the right thing to the wrong people. They are paid for their backs and hands, not their brains. They are general laborers who do what they're told. Not exactly how Wayne wanted to use his bachelor's degree.

Each day Wayne would open the door of the man-camp trailer to check the weather. It was always the same – cold, windy, gray. That meant long underwear and heavy insulated coveralls. The steel-toe boots, gloves, hard hat, and safety glasses were mandatory.
~~~

After the shift was over Wayne and Larry dumped their dirty, bulky winter clothing on the floor of their room and headed for the showers. Wayne's strategy was to shower first-thing, so he wouldn't have to see the other naked oil workers swinging their dicks. Everybody was dirty. Men caked with drilling mud, oil splatter and grease. It took intense scrubbing with Lava pumice soap to get it off the skin.

After a shower it was dinner and a quick return to the room to get some sleep.

But sleep had consequences – the nightmares of the Kelly Spinner. Wayne had recurring dreams of getting caught in the spinner and spun around. He would wake up screaming.

After a few weeks of drilling the Lateral was completed. Water trucks lined up to pump their brackish fluid in a holding tank. Roustabouts weren't needed at this point so Wayne sauntered up to a parked water truck to chat with the driver.

"How ya'll doing?" asked the driver.

"Yeah, fine. Another day another dollar, you know," said Wayne.

"Are you waiting to pump out?" Wayne asked.

"No this is the chemical line. They pump chemicals into these tanks before we off-load," the trucker replied."

"What kind of chemicals? They told us it was only water," Wayne replied.

"Yeah, it's ninety-nine percent water; the rest is hazardous chemicals. You know the one-percent," the trucker answered. "Just like the super-rich in America. You never see 'em, but you know they're there."

"What kind of chemicals?" asked Wayne.

"Well, there are acids, chloride, benzene, ethylene glycol, isopropanol. Nobody really knows how many chemicals are in this fracking fluid, because the data is not published," the driver explained.

"What about the EPA?" Wayne asked. "They monitor the drinking water standards for the county. They must have approved what goes in the wells."

"Not out here they don't," the trucker recoiled. "In 2005 the Bush-Cheney administration rammed through what's called the Halliburton Loophole. Basically they pushed through an energy bill that exempted the fracking process from the 1974 Safe Drinking Act."

"Many of these chemicals are toxic to humans. Ethylene glycol is a bad guy; it's toxic to the central nervous system, the heart and kidneys. The reason I know that is I have a cousin who de-ices planes for Delta. They use the same chemicals in the de-icing process. Anyway, he's sick from the shit. So don't get any of that water mist in your lungs," the trucker said.

"Well that's nice to know. Nobody said anything to me about toxic chemicals. Here I thought my main concern was getting my arm ripped off by the Kelly Spinner. Now I have to worry about the air I breathe," Wayne said.

"How the hell do you know all this?" Wayne asked.

"I used to be a high school chemistry teacher. So I was tuned in to the chemical aspects of the process. When the Texans got elected to the White House, I knew those fuckers were going to corrupt the process - and they did," the trucker stated.

"Let me guess; you were a teacher in Texas, voiced your opinion and found yourself out of a job," Wayne asked.

"It wasn't my opinion that got me in trouble – it was my dick! I had sex with a few of the girls on the softball team I was coaching. One of the mothers found out I was banging her daughter and she got me fired. Lucky for me, in the state of Texas, the age of consent is seventeen; otherwise I'd be in prison," the trucker said proudly.

"I'm trying to earn enough money on this water trucking job to go back to school and get my Ph.D. Then I can teach at a community college somewhere and fuck all the young coeds I want," explained the trucker with a smile.

"Well good luck with that," Wayne said as he walked away.

~~~

Jerry clicked away on his computer keyboard when he heard the call on the *Daily's* police scanner.

Explosion at the Juniper gas station. All fire and police please respond.

He bolted from his chair, grabbed his cell phone, scanner and the keys to the Ford Focus. When he arrived
~~~

at the station he was thrilled to see action and a wonderful story unfolding.

In the side parking lot, a 32-foot RV was completely ablaze. Half of it was burned through and the fire was raging all over it. The fiberglass skin was almost completely melted off the sides, leaving only some remnants of the aluminum superstructure. He grabbed his camera and took a dozen photos from different angles as fireman hosed down the stinking, toxic mess.

Jerry saw cop Marky-Mark keeping bystanders away, so he approached and took a picture of him standing in front of the fire.

"What the hell happened? Anybody hurt?" Jerry asked.

"Typical situation. This out-of-state dumb-ass came up here to work. Pulled in here to eat and sleep. When he started his propane stove it exploded. He probably didn't soap his gas lines, so the propane was leaking out, building up in the interior," said the cop.

"Is the guy hurt?" Jerry asked.

"He's a bit cooked, but he'll be all right. They rushed him to the hospital. It's just flash burns. His hair will grow back. His fucking Shi Tzu dog wasn't so lucky. Dog didn't get out; now he's a crispy critter," Mark laughed..

Jerry returned to the *Daily* to download his pictures and write up the story. As he walked into the building he heard a woman yelling at Gloria.

"This newspaper is responsible for the validity of the

ads you run," she yelled. "I'm not leaving here until I talk to the publisher."

Jerry stepped up to the counter. "Is there anything I can help with?" he asked meekly, not really wanting to step-in-it.

"Well yes there is," the woman raged. "You can reimburse me $1300 dollars for the puppies I purchased from an advertisement in this newspaper."

"I don't understand," Jerry replied.

"I answered a classified ad printed in the *Daily* for a litter of six bulldog puppies. I paid $1300 dollars by Western Union to Fred Roberts on Broadway – which is just down the street. Well guess what? I never got the puppies and there ain't no Fred Roberts on east Broadway. I've been scammed out of my money because this fucking newspaper is printing bogus ads," she ranted.

"That's a raw deal," Jerry sympathized. "Have you talked to the police? Maybe they can trace the money to an account."

"Oh yeah, I talked to that asshole Mark Janson. You know what he said to me? He said, 'How could you be so stupid?'" she sneered. "I don't like that guy, and I don't like this paper. You tell Ditzy I want to talk with her."

"She's not around today. She's probably out riding horses," Gloria said calmly.

"Well, you give her my contact information. I've had enough of this shit for one day, and I need a drink," she said and stormed out the door.

Jerry looked at Gloria. "Why wouldn't she go pick up the puppies in person if they were in town?"

"Well, she's either dumb as a brick or she's a scam artist," Gloria said as she returned to her desk.

~~~

Lisa had never seen so much money in her life. The oil men were flush with cash and with so little time off, when they did come into Williston for some fun, they spent their money freely.

She worked the pole every day, whatever shift was available. Lap dance after lap dance. Her legs were getting raw from sitting on all the Carhartt. She bought a tennis bag to hold the money she scooped off the stage. Her only worry was getting to her car when day was over. She carried around $500 dollars every day. Working the day shift was no problem, but at night, there were men lurking in the shadows, smoking behind dumpsters, doing meth and smoking weed. She gave Sergio the bouncer a twenty to escort her to the Jetta. His three-hundred pound body parted the dregs like a snow plow blasting through drifts.

"Hi Jerry," Lisa said as she walked into the kitchen. "What's for dinner?" she laughed, knowing Jerry's talent with a stove. "That smells great, what is it?"

"How's my favorite stripper?" Jerry asked. "How much did you make today? Another thousand?"

"I did okay. The guys were pretty generous," she said, as she picked up celery a stalk that was cleaned and laying by the sink.
~~~

"Help yourself to my food," Jerry said, "what's mine is yours."

"You're such a smart-ass. Okay, I'll get groceries tomorrow, then I will cook for you. I bought some wine," she said as she pulled two big bottles of white wine from a paper sack.

"That will go great with the garlic-shrimp-mushroom alfredo I'm making," Jerry said. "Open one up and let's get drinking."

"Right-on," Lisa said, "it's way past beer-thirty."

They ate dinner in the back yard, on the little porch that overlooked a small, fenced in yard with a birdbath.

"I used to camp in the Boundary Waters in Minnesota," Jerry said. "You canoe into the wilderness and bring everything with you. You eat outside, sleep in a tent in whatever weather comes in. Sometimes it's great, sometimes it rains for days on end. But no matter what the condition, food always tastes better when you eat outside," he said.

"We use to camp in Colorado," Lisa replied. "I know what you mean. In the mountains the air is clean and crisp and the elevation makes you feel more alive."

"Won't be long and this won't be an option. We're going to have sub-zero and snow pretty soon. We should probably get a bird feeder out here so we can watch birds and squirrels while we look out the window," Jerry sighed.

Lisa stretched out her long legs and groaned a bit as she laid them on the chair across from her. Jerry could see her strong leg muscles rippling against the black stretch pants she had on.

"Your feet are sore; give me a leg," he said, as he patted his thigh like he was coaxing a pet.

She gave him a funny, sideways glance and then slowly lifted a leg and set it on his lap.

Jerry took off her shoe and slowly, started a firm but gentle foot massage. Instantly, Lisa started groaning with pleasure and closed her eyes.

"Oh my god that feels good. I had no idea my feet were so sore," she said. "Those spike-heel shoes are trashing my feet."

"Give me your other foot," he asked, and she quickly set the other leg on his lap.

With a foot in each hand he worked the bottoms, inside each toe, tugged on each toe until they popped and then slowly started one hand up her calf muscle. He could feel the solid muscle of her legs, the results of dozens of bends she did on the pole, hour after hour. She was more than hard, she was ripped.

Her face blissful, her mouth was open.

Suddenly she opened her eyes and stiffened. "You've got to stop. You're making me horny."

Jerry smirked, pleased that he had taken her that far. "Okay. We don't want you to get all horned up now. I'm sure it would be really hard for you to get laid in this town," he laughed.

She looked at him with devilish eyes. "If I want to get laid I wouldn't have to leave the house," she countered.

"Oh, touché. Now you're getting me all hot-n-bothered," Jerry teased.

"Time for me to watch Thursday night football," Jerry said, as he got up and put the dishes in the sink.

~~~

Williston cop Mark Janson walked into the Mayor's office.

"Hey Marty, I think you should come over to the jail sometime today. There's a guy there I want you to meet," Mark said.

"What's his story?" ask Fitzgerald.

"We arrested him last night outside the strip club for pissing in the street. He came into town on a Greyhound bus from Aspen, Colorado. Today he's telling me that Aspen bought him the ticket to come up here. Evidently they're getting rid of their homeless indigents by giving them bus tickets to Williston," the cop spat out.

"I checked for outstanding warrants in Colorado and he has a long and checkered past for trespassing, open container of alcohol, disorderly conduct and menacing," Mark said. "I don't think he's bullshitting about the free bus ticket."

"I'll come over there right now and have a talk with this fella. If those assholes in Aspen are sending us their problems, then we're going to have to return the favor,"
~~~

Fitzgerald said calmly.

Marky-Mark escorted a 30-year old dead-beat, dressed in blue-n-white stripe inmate clothing, into the visitor room. The Mayor was already there waiting to question him.

"How are you," said the prisoner, "My name is Jimmy Smith," he offered his hand but the Fitzgerald ignored it.

"Sit down and tell me your story," the Mayor stated bluntly.

"Well, I was living in Aspen and they bought me a bus ticket to come up here. I was like, on that bus for two days and had a bit of money in my pocket. When I got off the bus I needed to let off some steam, and I got in trouble. I was only here for like half a day and I ended up in jail and I didn't even do nothing wrong. Like whoa, welcome to Williston Jimmy. I think I had too much to drink at the strip club and I was arrested for pissing in the street, but I can't remember. They didn't tell me what I'm charged with," Jimmy stated.

"What do you do for a living?" asked the Mayor.

"Well I don't really have a career. I travel with my backpack from town to town. I stay and work for a month and then I keep moving. See this tattoo on my neck? It's an outline of the lower forty-eight. I've been walking across the country now for four years. I get a little red dot tattooed inside this tattoo for everywhere I been," he said proudly.

"I was actually going to Minnesota, so if somebody wanted to do that, buy me a ticket to the Twin Cities, they could get 'er done, you know what I mean? Cough up the money for ticket and some grub and I'll be on my way to see Minneapolis," he offered.

"Otherwise I'll probably stay here. There's an oil worker in my cell who has a good lead for me to find work. But I don't want to stay where I'm not wanted. I know how small town cops are," he said, looking sideways at Marky-Mark . "Once you're on the cop's radar they're always watching."

"Wait here a moment, while I discuss this with the law enforcement officer," the Mayor said as he got up from his metal chair. The cop followed him out of the room and into the hallway.

"I think it's best if we get this goof-ball out of town the same way he came in. I don't want to get into a pissing match with Aspen, sending these deadbeats back-n-forth, so let's get him on a bus to Las Vegas. Once he's in Vegas he'll disappear into the homeless area around Fremont Street and we'll never see or hear from him again. I'll take money from the contingency fund for the bus ticket and give him an extra hundred bucks. Make him sign a release agreeing to take the bus ride if he leaves jail," the Mayor instructed.

Marky-Mark said nothing, but kept nodding his head in agreement.

"Make sure he gets on the bus," Fitzgerald commanded.

~~~

The Williston City Council was called to order by
~~~

Mayor Fitzgerald.

"Tonight's agenda has been posted so we will begin with the first item on the list, which is the request from Argeant LLC to build several retail stores with transient work crews from out of state," Fitzgerald stated.

Councilman George Brekke spoke first.

"These companies have a desire to build retail stores within Williston. This is a benefit to the community as a whole. I propose that we allow these types of projects to go forward with a mandate that the work crews must reside on the job site. It will be the responsibility of the contractor to provide for their on-site lodging with trailers."

"We will need an ordinance drafted," said councilman Cybak. "So that we can enact and enforce the rules of governance. Otherwise there will be problems," he spouted.

Fitzgerald spoke up, "Perhaps we should enact a moratorium on all construction within Williston until we get ordinances drafted."

The threat of a moratorium will make me a lot of money.

"I agree," said Cybak, "these issues shouldn't be thrown on our backs; let the developers figure this out. They can plan it out and then submit it to us for approval."

"We have additional housing already approved and being constructed. In the next few months some twelve hundred new housing units will be opened," Fitzgerald stated. "This would be a good time for us to examine how fast we want to grow as a community. We don't want too much too soon, too little too late."

"We don't need a moratorium; isn't that a bit harsh?" asked Brekke. "Let's look at these on a one-by-one basis."

"Very well," said Fitzgerald. "For now, we will look at these requests individually, but if the requests get overly complicated then I see no alternative than to draft restrictive ordinances to control the manner in which these build-outs occur."

"Which brings us to our next order of business. The violations of the Nabors man-camp on 58th street. I'm going to ask Williams County building inspector Karl Horton to come forward and give us an update," Fitzgerald said.

Horton, a lanky cowboy-type with a big silver belt buckle strode forward to the lectern.

"A violation and stop-order was issued against the owner of the man camp for operating twenty-six units, on the property for thirty-one days. The ordinance calls for fines of $500 per day per unit, which is $13,000 per day for all the units, totaling $390,000 dollars. Plus the $35,000 building permit fee which is doubled due to the circumstance. So the grand total is $461,000 dollars."

"Let this be lesson to them and to any other builders who disregard the planning and zoning regulations of the county," voiced Cybak.

"Mr. Horton," asked Fitzgerald, "are there other possible violators in the region?

He smelled money.

"We have three or four more that are being served notice, but we're only scratching the surface. What we really need is to hire a dedicated compliance officer," Horton stated.

"With these hefty penalties, I think we can afford to hire someone to attend to this need. I'll discuss the issue with the city manager next week. We can probably hire a contractor so we can avoid paying health insurance and retirement costs," Fitzgerald said.

"The next order of business is a request for exemptions from the city-wide truck and trailer parking ban for several fast food businesses," Fitzgerald calmly read aloud. "Appearing before us is Steve Snell, the manager of Hardee's. He is also representing several other fast food businesses in this matter, including McDonalds, Pizza Hut, and Country Kitchen."

Snell stepped to the microphone to plead his cause.

"As you all know there is a lack of housing in Williston. The restaurants in this town as well as many business are just trying to survive. Our companies have had to rent RV's and park them in private lots with an average cost to us of $8,000 a month. It's sad to see people sleeping in cars. We have three motor homes, pop-up campers and people sleeping in vans. We may have to purchase a house in Williston just to house our workers. Our franchises have no ability to help our workers with lodging. If the city of Williston values our franchises, than we ask for a temporary dispensation for fast-food workers to park their vehicles in the city of Williston for the next six months, until additional housing units become available," Snell stated.

"Well that's an interesting situation," Cybak said, "but when are these businesses going to realize that they need to make a plan for employee housing, before they construct fast food businesses in Williston? This is not our problem. This is their problem. Perhaps these employee housing plans will have to be part of any future building proposals that come before the planning and zoning commission. Your problem is not a Williston problem; it's a problem for McDonalds and the last time I looked, McDonalds stock was trading for $80 a share. Perhaps a mega-corporation like that would pony up for employee housing."

A gray-haired woman in the audience stood up and yelled at Cybak,

"Is that how you feel about senior citizens too? Tough luck for us? The rent for my apartment has been seven-hundred a month for the past six years. I just got notice of increase for the next lease to two-thousand a month. What am I to do? Other than move out of town, along with all the other elderly citizens who can no longer live in our home community," she barked.

"Well there's nothing I can do for you Mrs. Nordstrom, I feel bad for you and those in your situation but this is how capitalism works. If you own rental property you charge whatever the market will bear. I know it's a raw deal for some, but it's a very good deal for investors and property owners," Cybak responded.

"You are one cruel and heartless bastard," she yelled

at him. "Allowing the elderly of Williston to be thrown out of their homes, just so some greedy landlords can line their pockets. It's just not right. You have the power on this committee to write an ordinance to prevent this from happening, and yet you sit there on your hands, tongue tied, pretending there is nothing you can do."

Fitzgerald picked up the gavel and banged it on the table. "Let's return to our agenda for the evening. We're getting a bit off-topic here."

The council watched as Mrs. Nordstom stormed from the room, her large purse swinging and banging into things as she departed.

Fitzgerald noticed the two Texans in the audience. They had slipped in unnoticed during the session.

Did they have the suitcases?

Forty minutes later the meeting was adjourned. Fitzgerald checked his phone and saw a message from the Texans. They wanted to meet at the usual spot.

He pulled up behind their rental car.

"How you boys doing?" he asked as he approached their car on foot.

"It's fucking cold up here; that's how we're doing," said the short guy.

"Well then, no need for small talk. Let's get down to business," Fitzgerald said with a serious tone.

Show me the money.

The tall Texan opened the trunk. Fitzgerald saw two small briefcases, one black and the other green. Tex pulled out the black case and opened the latches and the lid.

"Oh that is pretty," Fitzgerald said as he looked at the three gold bars recessed in red felt. "I'm going to have to hold them when I get home; kinda like a woman's titties aren't they? You just want to get them out and put your hands around 'em."

The Texans were not amused.

"When can we expect the variance to go through?" asked shorty.

"That other case has the cash-money?" asked Fitzgerald.

"Yes," said the stubby Texan.

"Well, we have another meeting on the calendar in two weeks. I'll have that item placed on the agenda and barring any unforeseen circumstances, we should be able to push through your site exemption at the meeting."

"Make it happen. We're only interested in results, not excuses or delays," growled stubby.

"Now boys, you need to have some faith in your fellow man," Fitzgerald said in a Struther Martin voice. "We don't have to be friends, but we can establish a good working relationship based on *quid quo pro*, right?"

"We will be back in two weeks," said the tall Texan.

"I'll see you then, and I hope to find you boys in better

humor next time," said Fitzgerald, keeping the Struther Martin thing going.

The Texans drove off. Fitzgerald placed the suitcases in the front seat and pulled out his one-hitter for a toke, and looked up at the night sky. There was no snow on the ground yet, but the brutal winter was just around the corner.

~~~

Winter hit Williston on Veterans Day in November. Snow and sub-zero cold arrived a month early. An Aleutian Island hurricane pushed snow and cold into Canada, down into the Dakotas. A foot of snow fell in one day, covering everything from Billings to Minneapolis. Roads closed, flights were cancelled and work nearly stopped on the drilling rigs as men and machinery had difficulty operating in the frigid conditions.

The man-camp bus shuttled the crew to the rig as usual, but Wayne and Larry were unsure of the day's agenda.

The rig manager, Gene, approached them when they got off the bus.

"I need you fellas to drive truck today. You both have CDL's right?" he asked.

They grunted affirmative and nodded their heads.

"I need you to drive dump trucks to the Williston landfill. You don't need any endorsements or permits. With this nasty weather, we're going to hold off on new drilling for a few days. We're going to repair equipment
~~~

on the rigs and get rid of frack sand waste. In a couple of days, when this weather blows over, we'll get back to drilling," he instructed.

"So I need each of you to fire up a dump truck, head over to the sediment tank and get loaded up with hot sand," he said.

"What do you mean hot sand?" asked Larry.

"It has low levels of radioactivity so it needs to go in a landfill," Gene replied.

"How low? Do we need special suits or gloves for protection?" Wayne asked, with a skeptical look on his face.

"These are naturally occurring radioactive substances from underground – Uranium 238, Thorium 232, Radium. Our radiation exposure is insignificant. No toxicity at all. Even the federal government doesn't regulate it, so it must be safe, right?" he stated with a big grin.

"Yeah right," said Larry.

The rig manager walked away and the two roustabouts looked at the dump trucks.

"Do you want the blue one or the blue one?" Larry asked.

"I want the blue one with the good heater," Wayne replied.

They climbed aboard the trucks and started them up. Wayne was impressed that the cab was actually clean; Larry was impressed there was a radio that worked. Both trucks had heaters that kicked out hot air.

A front-loader filled the trucks with sediment-sand and they drove out of the rig area. Wayne's mind was loose; he felt relief, doing something different than the normal, grueling routine.

This was going to be an easy couple of days. Time to relax a bit, heal the body.

The roads were in poor condition. Trucks and cars were scattered here and there in the ditch. The heavy dump trucks had great traction so they were in no jeopardy of spinning out of control and leaving the road. Wayne ran his hand through his hair. It felt thick and dirty; he looked in the mirror and saw a stubble-faced, tired-guy looking back at him.

How long can I keep this up?

Winter was just setting in and he was feeling worn out. Maybe the exhaustion would dissipate. Maybe guys just pushed through it until your body toughened up. He wasn't sure. He was sure about the money. He was making bank and that was reason enough to keep slogging forward.

The Williston landfill was on the outskirts of town. They drove past the open yellow gate, up onto the scale to get weighed. He wasn't sure if they charged by the ton or the load. It didn't really matter, he wasn't paying for it. The gal running the scale opened the sliding glass window of the scale shack.

"What company?" she asked.

"Continental," Wayne yelled back. "Do you charge by the load or by the ton?"

"I have no idea," she said. "I only run the scale and the Geiger."

"Can you pull up over there and park, I'll weigh the second truck and then I'll check the load," she asked.

Check that load, what was that about?

"Okay," Wayne said, as he put the truck in the granny gear and crept off the scale.

Larry weighed in and pulled his truck behind Wayne. They got out of their trucks and pulled their Carhartt hoodies up over their ears.

It's fucking cold out here.

The gal walked out the scale-shack with a detector device in her hands. She turned it on, zeroed it out with some buttons and held up the plastic, pie-plate sized sensor to the dump truck box and swept it over and over, up and down from the rear of the truck to the front of the truck.

"Uh-oh," she said, "this load is hot."

She walked to Larry's truck and repeated the same procedure.

"Yup, they're both hot. I'm afraid you guys can't dump here. These loads exceed the maximums allowed," she said.

"What do you mean they're too hot?" asked Wayne.

"The material exceeds the regulations for NORM – Naturally Occurring Radioactive Material. Anything above five picocuries-per-gram is too high. We call that a hot load," she said.

"Our boss told us this is naturally occurring material from the earth," Larry said. "Not dangerous to anyone."

"He's kinda right; it is naturally occurring. But when you pull it out of the ground from thousands of feet below the surface, the toxic concentrations go way up. This stuff is definitely hazardous to human health," she stated.

"What do we do now?" asked Wayne. "Is there another landfill nearby that accepts hot loads?"

"No, not in this state. This is a North Dakota guideline, so you won't find anywhere to dump this load legally," she said.

"What do you mean legally?" Wayne asked.

"I don't ask, so don't tell. This Geiger counter finds about twenty hot loads per week. I have no idea where you guys are dumping this stuff. And I don't want to know, it's none of my business," she replied.

"Sorry guys," she said and she returned to the warmth of the scale shack.

They returned to the drill rig and told Gene what had happened. He just nodded his head; he wasn't surprised.

"That's okay. We have a private contractor who will take the hot loads. Let me give him a call and see if he's around today. This weather might be causing some issues," he said as he pulled out a cell phone from his bibs. He twirled around to get out of the wind, took off his sunglasses so he could read the phone dialer and pressed an autodial button.

"Hello Elmer, this Gene at Continental. Are you okay with some of my men bringing a couple loads today? You are, okay, good. I'll send 'em down the road, they'll be there in a couple hours," he said as he snapped the phone shut.

"Okay we're good to go. I'll give you directions to the rancher's location. I need to get you some cash. He only takes cash. Hang on while I go to the job shack," said Gene.

After ten minutes he came back, handed Wayne an envelope, thick with cash.

"There's two thousand dollars in there. Make sure you count it out to him and Larry I need you to watch the transaction," Gene said.

"Is there something shady about this guy?" asked Wayne.

"Elmer Hayes is just a rancher who needs money. Nothing shady, just an honest business transaction that needs to be on the up-and-up. We can't pay him with a check so it's important that the transactions are witnessed," Gene stated.

"Oh, he doesn't want the taxable income. I get it," Wayne said.

"Something like that," replied Gene. "Better get going, eat your lunch on the way. He's a couple hours from here and with the roads the way they are, you'll only get one load today."

Two hours later, after a stop at Subway for a $15 foot-long sub-sandwich, the two trucks pulled into a run-down prefabricated ranch house in the middle of nowhere, North Dakota. A chubby guy came out of the home and approached the trucks. Wayne and Larry got out to meet him.

"Hey boys, glad you made it out here. This weather is so shitty I wasn't sure you'd make it," he said. "You got the money?" he asked, licking his lips.

Wayne gave him a once-over inspection.

The dude looks like Oliver Hardy of the Laurel & Hardy comedy duo.

"Yes, right here," Wayne said as he pulled the envelope out of his pocket. He grabbed the stack of bills and counted out the hundreds. He counted twenty and handed the money to the rancher.

"Ah, this is my kind of Johnny-Cake," the rancher laughed.

"That's cornbread right?" asked Larry.

"Let's dump your load," said the Oliver Hardy look-alike.

"That's what she said," Larry laughed. Elmer didn't understand.

They climbed aboard the trucks and started down a field road that had been plowed by a tractor. Then turned into an open field with a gully running through it.

"Just back up to the gully and pull the cord," said Elmer.

They dumped their loads and drove out the way they came.

"What do you do with that stuff?" asked Wayne as he neared Elmer's house.

"Nothing, it just sits there and dries in the hot summer sun," replied Elmer.

"Outta sight, outta mind," said Wayne.

"You got it," replied Elmer as he climbed out of the dump truck.

"Drive safe boys, them roads is a pain-in-the-ass," he said as he waddled back to his house.

Wayne pondered.

Was that legal? Moral? Ethical?

CHAPTER III

"This lady is missing," Marky-Mark said to Jerry as he handed over a color photo.

"What do you mean she's missing?" asked Jerry.

"Lori Haines went for her daily six-a.m. jog and never came home," Mark replied.

"Do you think she ran off with some guy? Lots of these gals get in fights with their men and run off with somebody else," Jerry asked.

"She's married, with kids. Oh, she's also a high school English teacher. So no, I don't think she voluntarily ran off with someone," Mark said with more emotion in his voice.

"In fact, I think she was abducted by some fuck-head oil worker and he's raping her right now in his truck or trailer," he said, his eyes getting narrow.

"What's next?" asked Jerry.

"Ask Ditzy to run this photo of her in the paper. The FBI will be here tomorrow to run the case. Kidnapping is federal," said Mark.

"She's out jogging in the middle winter? Jogging in January? She must be a marathon-runner type who just has to run, no matter what," Jerry said.

"So if she's not a captive of some asshole, she's likely frozen stiff in the ditch or in a dumpster," Mark said with a scowl. "We're organizing volunteer search parties.

Gonna fan out on every street and block; every alley, every dumpster. If she's in Williston we will find her. But if not, with her picture in the paper, maybe somebody will recognize her and give us a tip. That's all we have to go on right now," Marky sighed.

"Any clues at all? Husband have any ideas?" asked Jerry.

"Yes, but keep this to yourself. We found her running shoe on the street," Mark said.

"She lost her shoe? Nobody runs on the snow and ice without a shoe. That can't be good," Jerry replied.

"Right, but we don't want to create a panic. On the other hand, if there's some jerk-off out there, stalking and kidnapping women, we need to alert the community. So this thing is going to get big in a hurry," Mark said as he turned and left the *Daily*.

For the next two weeks, hundreds of searchers joined the police in the hunt for the missing woman. The National Guard came out, canine units, helicopters and airplanes kept searching a larger and larger radius. Then the weather turned sub-zero, heavy snows fell, and people started to give up. If she had been nearby they would have found her.

Paranoia set in. **People Are Monsters** billboards went up, depicting creepy, shadowy men, lurking around every corner. Fear-selling was rampant. Carpetbaggers flooded the city selling alarms systems, handguns out of their trunks, and concealed-carry instructors held packed classes every Saturday in the VFW basement. Business was booming in the fear sector.

It didn't take long before a politician arrived. The self-serving scoundrel was looking to garner free publicity by holding public meetings so his constituents could voice their concerns. In reality, it was all about getting face time and polishing his public image.

Senator Curt Konrad approached the podium in the city hall and looked out at the audience of citizens and civic leaders. Wearing an expensive suit with color coordinated red tie and the obligatory stars-n-stripes button on his lapel - in case someone doubted his national allegiance - began his oratory.

"This meeting was actually organized before Lori Haines went missing. Her abduction further illustrates the need for coordinated efforts between federal, state, and local law enforcement agencies in this fight," he stated. "We are trying to streamline coordination between all the resources available – the FBI, the DEA, and the US Marshal Service."

He went on and on about nothing; the audience sat politely while he continued to blow hot air at them. When he ran out of pabulum, he turned the floor over to the county Sheriff.

The fat, grizzled Sheriff who had a hometown look compared to the slick bureaucrat put the audience at ease – *he was one of them.*

"Believe it or not folks, our biggest issue in the county is domestic violence. The calls have gone way up and there is very little we can do about it. We have more vehicle accidents and DWI arrests and not nearly enough officers to take care of the problems. In a word, we are overwhelmed with calls and understaffed," he complained.

"Like every other business in this area, we can't hire more officers because of the housing shortage. There is nowhere for them to live. We have the authority and budget to hire more officers but there's nowhere to put them. This shortage is causing retention problems with the officers we do have. They are over-worked and underpaid relative to their increased housing costs," he said, looking up at the audience for sympathy.

"We can't effectively recruit new officers either. Experienced officers, and those with families, won't come to Williston to live in a one-bedroom apartment for eighteen-hundred a month. This community needs to find a solution to the housing problem. Most of the crimes we see are at a local level, but to be sure, we are seeing drug-running, no-pimp prostitution, and illegal aliens."

The sheriff ended his talk and the senator jumped to the podium to get in the last word.

"My number one priority is to make your communities safer and bring the tools and resources of the state and federal government to help coordinate efforts and improve information flow so we can have stronger, better, more reliable law enforcement. Thank you for coming tonight," Konrad ended.

The audience grumbled a bit as they rose from their seats, but most people were pleased it was over so they could get home. It was cold and dark outside and some idiot had scheduled the meeting during Monday Night Football. The entire presentation was fluff.

Mayor Fitzgerald went home and turned on his gas

fireplace and his big flat screen television. The game between the Vikings and Bears was in the second quarter and it was still tied 10-10. He walked out to his garage and broke open the top of a cardboard box that held his precious new Cutty Sark - *Cutty Shark* as he liked to say at the tavern.

Fitzgerald needed the Vikings to cover by seven points. If they didn't, his three-team parley would be broken and his bookie in Las Vegas would need more cash. Every week he placed two hundred dollars on various three-team and sometimes four-team parleys that paid back six-to-one. He didn't need the money, the action just made the games on Sunday more meaningful. He was watching them anyway; why not have bets going.

He sat on his couch and opened up the suitcase the Texans provided. He took out each gold bar and held them, one-by-one, then together. They were beautiful and he wanted more. They were the perfect dimension to fit in his safe deposit box at the bank. He decided then and there to fill that long rectangle bank box with gold coins and bars. Untraceable, easy to trade, they could fit nicely in a boogie bag – in case he had to get out of town fast.

Getting out of town was on his mind. He could never be sure if one of these oil companies would turn on him, thrown him under the bus; some anonymous tip to the newspaper or the FBI. They could bring him down hard and fast. Other people would come out of the woodwork to pile on. The Texans were a bit surly. Maybe he was taxing their patience or pushing the greed-envelope too far?

He needed to sell his house – or suck the equity out

of it. It was nothing special, but it was worth a lot in the current Williston market. If it was in South Dakota it might bring $80,000; since it was in Williston it was worth $200,000. People would ask questions, but he could pretend he was trading up. Or better yet, say that he needed the money to move his hardware store to the new location. He pulled out his bag of weed from his stash-box and rolled up a joint. He would make a cash-out, refinance over the internet. No one in town would ever know. If the house sold, it sold. But if he had to leave town in a hurry, he would just walk away from it.

~~~

"The Amtrak train hit a semi?" exclaimed Gloria standing up from her chair. She kept the phone to her ear and looked at Jerry and waved him over.

"Let me put you on speaker phone," she said.

"Where did the accident happen?" Jerry asked.

"The crossing northeast of town," the anonymous caller responded.

"I'm headed out there," Jerry said as he returned to his desk.

He changed into his winter boots, grabbed his hat, gloves, camera bag and headed out the door.

When Jerry arrived at the scene he saw a semi-truck, sliced in two pieces. Police officers were getting a statement from the railroad engineer while the ambulance loaded up the injured trucker. Jerry took a few photos and waited for Marky-Mark to finish his police work.
~~~

"Hi Mark, what's the story," Jerry asked.

"Well, pretty simple to figure this one out. That jackass driving the water truck tried to beat the train across the tracks and lost. Fucker's lucky he ain't dead. If that train woulda hit the cab he'd be road pizza," Marky replied.

"Lucky thing he wasn't hauling oil or chemicals," Jerry said.

"Yeah good point. This would be a hazmat situation then. It's only a matter of time before something like that happens. I've never seen so many dumb-fucks in my life. Who the fuck can't wait for a fifteen car train to go by? It's not like this was a hundred-car train!" Mark said, shaking his head in amazement.

"Any leads on the missing school teacher?" Jerry asked.

"No nothing yet. But her body will turn up," Mark replied.

"What else is shaking around town?" Jerry asked.

"Have you seen the Walmart parking lot?" Marky asked. "It's empty."

"Empty?" Jerry asked.

"Yup, their management hired a private security firm to patrol twenty-four seven. No semi-trucks or campers are allowed to park in the lot for more than an hour. They can get supplies and then they have to leave," Marky said.

"They got tired of all the problems, I guess," Jerry said.

"Yes for sure. The place was looking like Hooverville. They don't need it. They get the business anyway; they don't need to accommodate transients," Marky said.

They both stood around while a flatbed tow truck backed up to the severed truck. Jerry looked at all the debris and litter in the ditches. Plastic bottles and fast food wrappers were everywhere.

"Hey Mark, do you guys ever write citations for littering?" Jerry asked.

"I'd like to. If I could catch any of those fuckers. Do you wanna know what the biggest litter item is? Fucking Gatorade jugs filled with piss," Marky said.

"Huh?" Jerry grunted.

"These truckers are stuck in traffic jams coming into town from both directions. Well they gotta take a piss and there's no way they can hold it or wait for a gas station. So they all keep these big plastic Gatorade jugs, the kind with the half-dollar size cap opening. They stick their dick in there and fill it up with hot piss, then chuck it out the window. They're all over here, up and down the road. Even the adopt-a-highway clean-up people won't touch 'em," he laughed.

"The country's gone to hell," Marky said with a smirk.

"Who said that, Rush Limbo?" Jerry asked.

"Nope, it was A-Number-1, the only hobo who could ride Shack's train," Marky said.

"Is that a movie?" Jerry asked, confused.

"Yeah, *Emperor of the North,*" Marky said.

"Okay then. Guess I'll have to watch that on Netflix so I'm in on the joke," Jerry said.

~~~

Wayne's thoughts kept going back to the radioactive waste dumping. It didn't seem like the honorable thing to do. He understood the reason for it. The oil company had to do something with the toxic sand, and the community of Williston had to protect their backyard. The oil companies that were making billions of dollars; it was their responsibility to deal with the waste in an ecological way.

Wayne looked around the drill site, determined to talk to Gene, the rig manager, about the problem. Gene wasn't around so he asked the Tim Hatchet, the driller, about the toxic sand.

"We hauled sand yesterday to the Williston landfill and they rejected it; said the radioactivity was too high. What's up with that?" asked Wayne.

"Well that happens from time to time. It probably didn't sit in the pond long enough," answered Tim.

"What's the pond?" asked Wayne.

"That retention pond right there," said the driller, pointing his finger to a ten-acre, rectangular area that had a berm pushed up on all sides.

"We pump the first tailings into that pond. The waste water and chemicals sit in that pond and evaporate the
~~~

VOC's, which stands for volatile organic compounds. The chemicals evaporate out into the air and leave behind the dirty sand that's pumped up from below ground. That's where the radioactive part comes from," he said.

"Yeah, I understand that. The ground has natural radioactivity, just like cinder block basements have radon emissions that are hazardous," Wayne said. "So these chemicals in the pond are released in the air. Does that contribute to acid rain and contamination of the air we breathe?"

"Well I wouldn't take your smoke break over there," Hatchet laughed. "I wouldn't eat my lunch downwind of that area either. You see, this is a dangerous operation. Getting oil or any natural resource out of the ground always has some side effects and environmental consequences. But in the end, it's always about money. You and I wouldn't have jobs; the cars need gas to run on. We have an opportunity for energy independence now; fracking will lower fuel costs for everyone. Lower fuel costs means more economic expansion, more goods and services can be produced and consumed. That's what makes the world grow round, buddy. Economics 1-0-1."

"Well, there's only a couple things wrong with your statement," Wayne said.

"This oil will get shipped to Texas, because that's where all the refineries are located. The Texans control Washington politics, they won't allow new refineries to get built—anywhere other than Texas or Louisiana. They make all the money on this. They extract it from North Dakota, they refine it into a gasoline in Texas, then they sell it on the international market," Wayne retorted.

"Oh yeah, how do you know all that?" asked Hatchet.

"That's what happened in the Alaskan pipeline. The oil that was pumped to Valdez was sold to Japan or anywhere off-continent that paid the highest price. That oil didn't remain in the USA; that was a lie told to the American people so they would support the endeavor. The oil companies who built the pipeline made all the profit from that oil. Oil that could have been nationalized for the good of U.S. citizens – just like this oil."

"Well keep in mind, the oil companies paid for that pipeline, not the government. They took all the risk and they got the reward. This ain't a socialist country, so don't start talking about nationalizing the natural resources like they did in Norway and Venezuela," Hatchet replied.

"We can agree on one thing – this is privately owned oil, making a few people and several companies very rich. The majority of Americans won't profit in any way from this extraction. In fact, there may be environmental consequences from doing this. Something that will last far beyond the two or three years this well is in operation," Wayne stated.

"Well, as long as I have a high-paying job, that's all that matters," Hatchet replied.

"Spoken like a true American," Wayne snorted. "As long as you get yours right?"

"That's the long and the short of it," said Hatchet as he put on his hard hat and returned to rig.

~~~
~~~

When Jerry returned home the house had the pleasant aroma of pizza. Lisa bounced around the kitchen in skin-tight leggings with a big sweatshirt that barely covered her butt.

"Hey girl," he said in his best African-American accent.

"Hey boy," she returned, with a smirk.

"That's inappropriate to call a man 'boy' you know," Jerry said.

"Oh is it now," she replied. "You guys can call us 'girls' and we just are supposed to be okay with that."

"Let's talk about you," Jerry said, wanting to change the direction of the conversation.

"Well, the pizza will be done in about ten minutes. I'm ready for some wine and a movie to go with the pizza," she said.

"Did you rent a movie when you bought the pizza?" Jerry asked.

"No, I thought you might have something on your computer," Lisa said.

"I could bootleg something from *thePirateBay* or we could watch Netflix; I've got someone else's login credentials. There's a movie I've been wanting to see that's probably on Netflix," Jerry stated.

"What movie?" she asked.

"A seventies movie, called *Emperor of the North.* It's about hobo's riding a train. Marky-Mark the cop told me it's really good," Jerry replied.

"Okay, I like seventies movies, as long as it's not too violent," she said.

"What's going on at the club?" Jerry asked.

"The word is out all over the country that there's big money up here. So girls are flooding into town. Some of the girls are experienced, some are not, but they're all getting booked. Which means I get less and less time at the pole, which means I make less and less money."

"We need another dance club in town," Jerry said.

"Not likely. There are too many bar fights and problems with patrons now. There's an old folks recreation center across the street. There's no way the city council will allow any more strip clubs in Williston," she said.

"If you know the right people, spread enough money around, anything is possible. Those politicians talk out of both sides of their mouths. As long as they get paid, most anything is possible," Jerry added.

"They're all corrupt?" she asked.

"No not necessarily corrupt, it's called *influence.* You can influence the outcome of political things if you throw money or favors around. Sometimes it's not about money but currying favors, or getting a chit."

"That's way beyond me. I take my clothes off for a living. I'll leave those things to you writer-types. I'm just a simple girl," she said in a southern-belle voice.

"Yeah right, simple girl getting filthy rich out here in

the boomtown," Jerry laughed.

"Speaking of money, when are you gonna pay some rent around here," he said joking.

"Oh, now its money talk. Cash or ass, nobody rides for free," she said.

"I'm just teasing you. Ditzy hasn't asked anything about you," he replied.

"Well that's good. Out-of-sight, out-of-mind," she said. "I'm not a freeloader. I'll make my first payment tonight after we watch the movie," she said as she slid the supreme pizza on the center of the table.

"Hmmmm, that looks really tasty," Jerry said.

Lisa came to his chair, flipped her leg over the chair and straddled him for a lap-dance. She put her arms around his neck and looked him in the eyes.

"It *is* tasty. You can taste it tonight," she said, staring right in his eyes.

~~~

"There's a body outside of town," Marky-Mark said as he walked into the *Daily*. "If you want to follow me Jerry, I'm headed out there."

"Is it her?" pleaded Gloria.

"Don't know; ain't seen the body yet," Mark said. "The call just came in. Someone saw it in the ditch."

Jerry took the Ford Focus and followed Marky's squad
~~~

car out of town. They headed west, towards the Montana border but stopped a few miles away. A Highway Patrol car was parked on the side of the road with lights flashing. The Williston squad car pulled in behind him, followed by the Focus.

The two cops knew each other and shook hands but the Highway cop glared at Jerry.

"He's with me," Marky said.

The three of them walked to the shoulder where the body lay. It wasn't her.

"Who the hell is this?" said Mark. "I was thinking it would be the school teacher."

"So was I," said the other cop.

They grabbed the male body by his jacket collar and yanked him up from the snow. The body broke free from the ice and they turned him over.

"Looks like some oil worker. Shot once in the chest and left in the ditch to die," said the Highway cop. "Let's see if you have any ID on you."

He dug around the man's coat pocket and came out with a check book.

"This will make things easier," the Highway cop said, as he opened the checkbook. "The victim's name is Lew Core."

Jerry took a few photos of the scene, but he knew there wasn't much of a story here. It *was* a murder scene but not *the* body they were hoping to find. He thought for a moment; not all crimes are equal, even though they were the same. The school teacher's abduction and probable death was front page news; this oil-worker guy was a nobody. A transient's death that nobody would care about – except his family, if he had any.

The highway patrolman went to his squad car and took out a body bag from the trunk. Jerry drifted back to his car and hopped back inside.

Fucking cold out here. Why the fuck do I live here.

As he drove the sixty miles back into town, he thought about things. Out here, far from Williston, life was frozen, quiet, peaceful. These people accepted physical suffering as part of their lives, it was contextual; it defined who they were as people. The invisible ranchers, hibernating like bears for the winter, waiting for the spring thaw. They accepted it, they lived with it, but he wasn't sure how.

A voice came over the hand-held police scanner.

Williston Fire Department, respond to Four Mile Corner for a fire.

Jerry stepped on the gas. He needed to make it there before they put out the blaze. For twenty miles he drove as fast as he could. The black smoke was visible for miles and as he pulled into the site and realized this was not an accident. A massive pile of pallet debris and plastic was ablaze.

A volunteer fireman directed traffic in and out of the area while the rest of the fire-crew pulled hoses and connected lines.

"What happened?" Jerry asked the fireman with the helmet stenciled "Buzz."

"Illegal burn. They said they were burning skids but there's a lot more in this fire than just skids. They were trying a controlled fire but it got out of hand. They're fucked now. They had no permit and there are toxins burning. You can smell it and see it in the smoke. Health Department will be involved on this one," yelled Buzz.

"There's a lot of material here. That pile is seventy-five yards long and twenty-five wide; it's going to burn a while," Jerry observed.

"Yup, and they're going to pay for everything, including the fire department's time, the clean-up, and then the fines," Buzz replied.

Jerry took a few photos and returned to his car.

Two action calls in one day. I love this job.

He drove back in silence to the *Daily*. He thought about how Lisa had fucked him silly the night before; how attracted he was to her, how dangerous she was for him. His feelings for her entwining his brain and body. He didn't know if he should resist and pullback or go all in, see where it would lead.

Heartbreak more than likely. Why get emotionally attached to a stripper? Don't be a dumb-fuck, pull out now!

He couldn't back away and he knew it. The carnival-ride would end when the music stopped. Another episode in life's rich pageant.

~~~

The city council meeting convened for the second time that month. Mayor Fitzgerald conveniently skipped the religious invocation and went right to the Pledge of Allegiance.

He had distributed the suitcases of money to the swing votes on the council; the variance for the Texan's oil storage facility on the edge of town was a slam dunk.

"The first item on the agenda tonight is an up or down vote on the Baker-Stewart facility which includes chemical storage warehouse, acid plant with mud-blending, and storage of explosives. We've had lengthy discussions with the company on this matter and they have assured us that all manner of safety regulations will be followed and the site will be secure and patrolled. This is a construction project of great importance and I feel that we should approve this site," Fitzgerald read from a script.

"You were singing a different tune a few weeks ago Mayor," injected Gaylor. "At that time you had grave concerns about the site being so close to town. Why the change of heart?"

"The simple fact of the matter is this. We are in the center of the greatest resurgence in oil production this country has had in our lifetimes. I want to side with economic expansion and job creation, rather than economic contraction, government restrictions and unemployment," Fitzgerald said.

"You feel free to vote your conscience on this, Mr. Gaylor. I won't be twisting your arm, or anyone else's arm
~~~

on this council," Fitzgerald added, trying to look sincere.

They took a vote and the resolution passed 4-3.

Easy, peasy, Japaneasy.

"Our next item on the agenda, Fitzgerald paused, "is a request to operate an adult-oriented business in the city of Williston by Sexxx-Kittty Corporation. The County attorney has informed me that Williams County Board has passed a restrictive ordinance banning these porn shops from the County; however, the City of Williston is exempt from that ruling. Is there any discussion on this topic?"

"I'm in favor of allowing this business entity," Cybak stated loudly, "as long as the proximately to schools and churches is within a respectful distance."

Fitzgerald swung his head to look at Cybak.

That fucker was getting paid off. Someone was calling in a chit or delivered a suitcase.

"I'm a bit surprised by your position," said Gaylor. "You're usually against anything that isn't hometown friendly or highly regulated by statute. Now you want to breeze through a pornography shop with no regulations attached to it? I'm starting to smell a rat."

"As the Mayor stated earlier, you are free to vote this issue any way you like Mr. Gaylor," Cybak retorted.

"Do you know what people see when they get off the Amtrak train at the depot?" Gaylor asked. "The first thing they see is the Queen of Hearts strip club. That's their first impression of Williston. Now you want to add more filth and smut to our town. What's wrong with you?"

Fitzgerald's mind was whirling.

That sneaky dog. Did Cybak back-channel the votes on this already?

Fitzgerald spoke up. "Would the council like to have a vote on this tonight or take this under consideration?"

"I think we should vote on this tonight," Cybak stated. "We don't need to push this out."

He did have the votes! They were all making money now. Everyone accept that dumb-fuck Gaylor.

The vote passed and they continued on.

"The next topic is the approval of contingency funds for the Williston library to hire two additional staff members and purchase ten more computers. The library is overwhelmed with oil workers using their computers. The library's core mission is to provide information and communication services to the public. This is a rather small budget item so I think we are all in agreement that the funds are available and the resources should be made available immediately," Fitzgerald read.

"All in favor say aye," Fitzgerald said

"Aye," they responded.

"Those opposed," Fitzgerald said. The room was silent.

"The ayes have it; request approved." Fitzgerald said.

"The next issue is the public access of the Raymond Community Center. There have been several incidents at the center and the staff has made a request for a change in the hours of operation," Fitzgerald said.

"Suzy Jones, the director of the Center is here to give us some information followed by members of the public who wish to speak," Fitzgerald said.

A young-looking 40-year old brunette, neatly attired in a business suit approached the podium to speak. Fitzgerald licked his lips as she walked up front. She was one hot-looking lesbian. He recalled trying to pick her up at the Old Saloon, but she shot him down. She preferred the crimson gash to the meat stick. This was his chance to *stick it to her for shutting him down.*

"I have the duty to report several unfortunate incidents to the council and the citizens here tonight. Three times in the past month staff members have found human feces in the shower area of the Raymond Center. Excrement has been found in more than one area, but all areas are highly used by members of the community. Such behavior is unacceptable, especially since toilets are only a few feet away. These actions cast a bad light on the people that are descending upon our community of Williston. It shows blatant disrespect for the facility, the people who use the facility and the community as a whole. It is a slap in the face," she continued.

"In reaction, to this and the outrage of parents in the community, fearing for the safety of their children, we have decided to close the community shower room to public access at two p.m. daily," Jones said. "We are also locking the internet access with a password, removing the lounge tables and the television, and prohibiting loitering in the commons area."

"We sympathize with the homeless job seekers who are respectful and clean up after themselves. But there are others who defecate on floors, steal electricity and put our community in danger," she intoned before taking her seat.

"Are there any members of the public who would like to speak?" asked Fitzgerald.

A man with a Carhartt jacket stood up, looked around briefly and approached the podium.

"My name is Clay Banacek. I have never written a letter to the editor, nor spoke in public on any issue. I have a degree in engineering and I work in the Bakken oil fields. I am an outsider. My work shift is 12-hours. Four a.m. to four p.m. I use the Raymond Community Center daily. I pay my three dollars to take a hot shower and shave my face. This week I was turned away. They told me the showers were closed to transients because of an incident," he paused to rub his eyes.

"I pay a per-day fee to use the facility, which is a public facility, supported by taxpayer-dollars. I pay state sales tax on all my purchases, a portion of which is returned to the city of Williston. I think this exclusionary policy of "locals only" reminds me of the "whites only" signs that existed in the South. Is that what you want here in Williston? This is discriminatory, so let's not confuse the issue. The real issue is very simple. Find the person who is shitting on the floor!" he yelled, as he walked away from the podium.

Applause went up from the audience as several other

oil workers were there to give their support.

"As they say, there are two sides to every story," Fitzgerald said. "I'm inclined to agree with the public on this issue. This is a tax-supported facility; there is also a user-fee. There is no reason to exclude or restrict users from a public facility based on assumptions. The real issue is criminal; we need to find the perpetrator who doesn't like using a toilet."

The other council members nodded in agreement.

"Ms. Jones, would you resume the normal hours of operation for the facility. No more discriminating against people either. Is that okay with you?" Fitzgerald said as he smiled. Jones' face went red. She had not seen this coming. Fitzgerald had bitch-slapped her in front of everyone.

"This meeting is now adjourned," Fitzgerald said.

CHAPTER IV

"We got a tip on the abduction," Marky-Mark said to Jerry over the phone.

"What kind of tip?" asked Jerry.

"A lady from Colorado called this morning. Says her boyfriend confessed to her on the phone. Said he and another guy grabbed Lori off the street and killed her. She said he was afraid and crying like a baby," Mark said. "We are looking for a Ford Explorer with Colorado plates. He's sleeping in his car; doesn't have gas money to leave town."

"We've got people out there looking for it. If we find him we will try to get a confession out of him," Mark said.

"I hope you guys find him and he fingers the other guy," Jerry said.

"Yeah, me too. If this guy can't carry his water, the other guy may kill him before we find him," Mark answered.

Three hours later they found the Explorer parked on a side street. Nobody was in the vehicle, so they parked squad cars on each end of the street to await the owner's return. An hour later a man in his twenties unlocked the truck and got in the back seat. Williston police immediately surround the car and put him under arrest.

They handcuffed him and sat him in the interrogation

room. Mark was pleased the Chief allowed him to conduct the interrogation. A video camera and tape recorder were rolling.

"Let's start from the beginning. What is your name?" asked Mark.

"Michael Reidell," he responded.

"Where are you from?" asked Mark. "How old are you?"

"Parachute, Colorado. I'm twenty-three years old."

"Do you know why you're in custody?" asked Mark.

"That lady that's missing. I didn't do it. It was Lester, he killed her," Reidell admitted.

Mark was stunned by the admission.

This guy is going to spill the beans.

"Tell me about it. What happened?" Mark asked.

"I drove up here from Parachute with Lester Williams. He's from there too. We come up here to get jobs on the oil wells. While we was driving, Williams made me smoke crack-cocaine the whole way up here. Then when we get to town, he's saying he wants to kidnap a woman and fuck her. Says the crack brings out the devil in him," he sputtered.

Mark sensed the man was a dunce, a real-time idiot of the sort you see in the movies; dumb, dumber, dumbest. He was in one of those categories.

"So we was driving through town and we see this lady jogging along the road and Lester tells me to pull over and stop. So I does. When she jogs up by the truck, Lester jumps out and grabs her and tries to push her into the back seat. But she won't go. She's kicking and punching, yelling. So Lester smacks her hard and drags her into the back seat. But she don't quit see," he looks up at Mark, like he should understand the dilemma.

"Lester just grabbed her by the throat to shut her up and choked her out. She died in the back seat. He never had sex with her or nothin'," Reidell trailed off.

"What happened next?" asked Mark.

"We drove to Walmart and bought some bread and baloney, 'cause we was getting hungry. And a spade shovel for digging a grave. I returned the shovel and got my money back," he said with a smile on his face.

Marky was certain now – this guy was a complete retard. He had the strongest desire to beat the snot out of him, right then and there.

"So you bought a shovel to bury her, then you buried her, and brought the shovel back with the receipt so you could get your money back," Mark said, trying to stay calm.

"That's right," said Reidell.

"Where did you bury her?" Marky asked.

This was important; a confession without a body could make for a sketchy trial and conviction. He needed one more bit of information for a *done deal.* They'd find that fuck-head Lester and have both the bastards behind bars. Maybe have the opportunity to execute them.

"We drove out of town and buried her behind a clump of trees, at the end of some field. Lester made me dig the hole, while he dragged her out of the truck. The ground was frozen solid, it was so hard to dig," Reidell explained.

"Yeah, with all the snow and cold I bet that was hard. Do you think you could point out the spot on a road map?" asked Mark.

"Hmm, no I don't really know where I was," said Reidell.

"Do you think you could find it again if I drove you out there?" asked Mark.

"Not sure. These roads all look the same to me," Reidell explained.

"Alright. Let's switch gears for a minute," Marky said, pausing for a moment.

"Tell me about this Lester guy. How old is he? Is he a criminal?" Mark asked.

"He's a bad guy. Probably about forty-five. I'm afraid of him. After he done killed that woman, he told me if I ever says anything about it, he would kill me and my family," Reidell said in a panic-voice.

"He sounds like a bad guy," Marky said. "Do you know where he is now? We should go find him so he doesn't hurt anyone else, including your family."

"I ain't seen him since that day. I got away from him

the first chance I had. I'm trying to get home to Colorado. I called my girlfriend and told her what happened, asked her if she could send me some gas money so I can get home," Reidell said with hyped emotion.

"So you haven't seen Lester Williams since that day?" asked Mark.

"I seen him once at Walmart. He was smoking outside with some guys, next to an RV," Reidell said, "but he didn't see me. I went in the store for some food and came out on the automotive side so he wouldn't see me leave."

"Do you think he was living out there at Walmart?" Mark asked.

"Maybe. He had a bunch of drugs with him. He probably traded some for a place to sleep in a camper. Or he found a job," he replied.

"Okay, we're done for now. But I want you to think about the spot where you buried that lady. It's really important that we find her. She has a husband and kids and they're worried. They want to have a funeral. You understand that right? You have a mom and dad and a girlfriend?" Mark asked.

"Is there a t.v. in jail?" Reidell asked. "I ain't watched t.v. in a month."

Marky met Jerry in the briefing room. He gave him a rundown of the situation.

"We need to find this other guy before we announce

anything. Can you write up an article about the arrest of these two guys, but keep it unpublished until we get this second guy. Be sure to mention that her body is buried in a shelter belt or line of trees on a property line near a road," Mark asked.

"This Williams-guy, he's probably a fucking snake who won't admit a thing and plead not-guilty. So we need to find that body. If we find the body, we can stretch his neck!" Mark said with great intent.

"Will do," said Jerry. "Thanks for bringing me in on this."

"How are you going to find this Lester guy since the RV's have vacated Walmart?" asked Jerry.

"They're still around town, up and down the streets, and some are in the RV lots. We'll get his photograph and show it around. We'll offer a reward if we have to. These transients have no love for each other, it's dog-eat-dog. They'll sell each other out for a pack of cigarettes," Mark said.

Mark was right. By the end of the day they had found Lester Williams.

~~~

The next day the headline of the *Daily* was in bold with photos of the suspects.
~~~

MUG SHOTS RELEASED

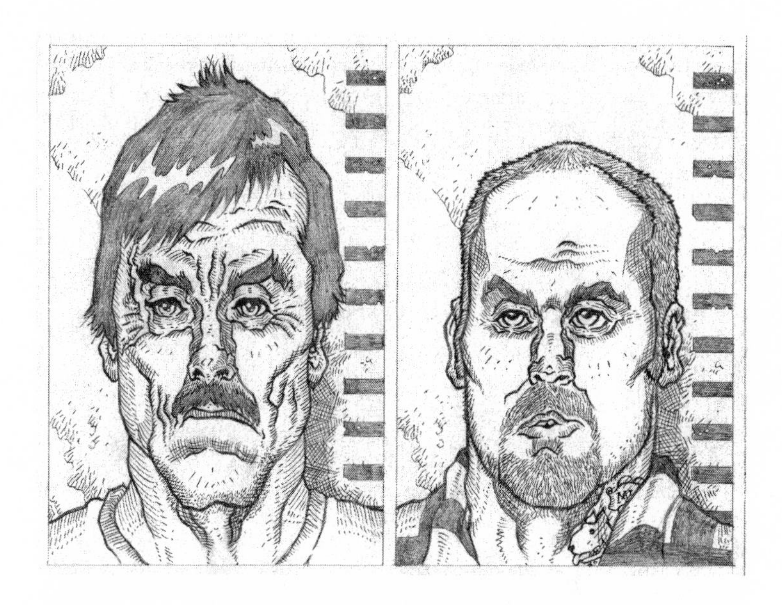

The paper revealed details of the crime, including backgrounds of both suspects to go with their photos. Authorities asked landowners to inspect their property for indications of a disturbance near "mature, dying or rotted trees."

As Marky predicted, Lester Williams wouldn't say a word. He was a hardened criminal, versed in the rule-of-law. He asked for an free attorney and denied any involvement in the disappearance of the missing woman. The judge set their bail at $2.5 million each.

~~~

Otto Van Horne took his Polaris 500 4-wheeler out for a drive along his fence line. He periodically checked his property boundaries to make sure his livestock were
~~~

where they should be and make sure no one had parked an RV on his land to make it their domicile. The wind on the prairie had dropped to nothing that morning, so he took advantage of the favorable conditions to buzz around his property. He loved riding the four-wheeler. He felt free and strangely effective and empowered as it pulled him up and down gullies and ravines, over the culverts and around stumps and obstructions. It was a marvelous invention and he was pleased that he had invested in Polaris stock. He had made 300% profit and the company's revenue kept going up.

As he rounded a tree line he saw it immediately.

Someone had been digging on his land.

He pulled up to the disheveled area, where unnatural dirt mounds pushed up against the snow.

The missing body, he just knew it.

The length of the soil disturbance was about four-feet by four feet; more of a circle than a trench. It made sense. The killers couldn't dig a traditional six foot long coffin hole; they simply dug a small pit in the ground and scrunched the body in a fetal position so they wouldn't have to dig very long.

He pulled out his cell phone and dialed 911.

Two hours later, an ambulance hauled away the body of Lori Haines. Otto watched as they removed her rock-hard body from the frozen ground. She was curled up like a sleeping cat. They set her on an oversized body-bag that looked like a poncho. He had seen dead GI's just like that during the Korean War. Men frozen solid with their arms akimbo and legs askew, like fallen puppets, laying splayed out on the ground. It brought back memories of the battle of Chipyong-ni in North Korea.

His mind flashed back; he was 19-years old and afraid. United Nations forces were surrounded by thousands of Chinese who advanced on them relentlessly. They mowed down the Chinks with machine guns and carbines, grenades and mortars. When the sun came up the next morning there were thousands of dead Chinese troops, frozen to the ground, looking up to the sky for some kind of answer, a redemption that never arrived.

The cold mornings were spent searching the dead Chinese bodies. The Chinks carried food rations and sometimes personal items – photos, letters – that were interesting to look at. Most of the GI's refused to search bodies; Otto had no problem with it. He enjoyed going through their pockets, the challenge was keeping his hands away from the bloody entry and exit wounds. Some of the troops thought it was ghoulish, but the officers wanted the bodies searched for intelligence documents – so Otto was assigned that task.

Otto took the field road home as fast as he could. After parking the ATV in the shed, he pulled out a heavy drink-glass and bottle of bourbon and poured four-fingers. He sat by the gas fireplace and slurped it down. He needed to clear his head. The nightmares of Korea would be visiting him.

~~~

The funeral was held in the high school gymnasium. The local churches were too small to accommodate the
~~~

thousands of people. Jerry sat on a cold metal chair, one of hundreds brought in for the event. Long, vertical purple-cloth banners hung from the walls to add sense of religious decorum to the empty, cinderblock walls. Flowers were everywhere, but there was no escaping the gymnasium atmosphere. The preacher stepped to podium that had EAGLES stenciled on the front.

"Our hearts are broken. This tragedy is Williston's 9-11 event. Yet God is still here. God is weeping alongside of us. God will turn death into life. Through Jesus, she will live again, as you and I will also live again. Hallelujah, Hallelujah," the preacher intoned.

Jerry had heard it all before; hundreds of times since the day he was born. He didn't believe a word of it. Where was God when *she* needed protection? Why did He *abandon* her in her moment of need?

Jerry looked around, glancing at the other faces in the room. Some people thought the same as he did; he could see the resolute indifference on their faces; *the preacher's words were poppycock.* Others, the true believers had the *I love Jesus* look on their faces. For them, this was salve for their wounds. They needed to make sense, of the non-sense. They needed to believe that something larger-than-life was in play, that some cosmic being was playing intelligent chess with their lives, and all the other humans on Earth. Gracing some, punishing others; the Believers needed assurance, re-assurance of Holy intervention in their daily lives. To face the abyss of nothingness, to not have and hold religious and spiritual context for life was unimaginable.

Jerry had never believed any of it, although he

tried to believe. From age five to fifteen, he was forced to attend Lutheran church every Sunday. The only thing he remembered about it was missing kickoff for NFL football games. There was no deity. He was certain of that every time he looked up at the stars in the Milky Way galaxy. He lived on a small blue planet on the edge of a small solar system, in a small galaxy that was only one among billions of other galaxies. There was no god coming to save him or anyone else.

He liked it that way. Being alone in the universe gave him perspective. Mortality meant you were born to die, but your time was yours do with as you pleased; for good, for bad, for ugly. Every person on earth was responsible for making their own footprints as they journeyed through life. Those who deluded themselves believing in an after-life were making a momentous error in thinking – fooled and brain-washed into believing in something that did not exist.

When the funeral was over he headed back home to Lisa. He needed a drink and some heart-pounding sex. It felt good to be among the living.

~~~

Lisa was home and she was horny. They banged the headboard for a half hour before they lay exhausted, staring at the ceiling.

"I don't know if I can do this much longer," she said.

"Why, what's happening," Jerry asked her.

"Hmmm, the money is dropping off because of all
~~~

the new girls. They're charging us to dance now. Can you believe it? But we don't have to tip-out anymore," she laughed. "They fine us if they smell weed in the backroom. The fine us if one of the girls takes a piss in a trash can."

"They piss in the trash cans?" asked Jerry.

"Sometimes they can't hold it. There's only one toilet in the whole place. It's a dumpy, shit-hole establishment," she said.

"I'm just tiring of it. My heart's not in it any more. I've put away fifty-grand. That's enough. I wanted a hundred because of my student loan debt, but…I'm not gonna make it," she stated.

"What's next then? You're not going to stay in town," he asked, feeling his heart sink in his chest.

"I don't know. I haven't thought that far down the road," she replied.

"What are you going to do? How long are you staying in Williston?" she countered.

"I don't know," Jerry said, "Winter is almost over now. I hadn't thought about the next job. Been so busy with this one," he said, realizing he hadn't thought about the next job at all.

"Have you ever been to Portland?" she asked.

"Nope, never been there. What's in Portland?" Jerry asked.

"I haven't been there," she said, "but it looks good on a

map – oceans, rivers, trees, seafood, Cascade Mountains."

"I think there are jobs there too. Lots of young people moving into the area. That's what I read on the internet. There's a community of like-minded people. You don't find that everywhere," she said.

"Take Williston," she said. "It's all the same; everyone is looking to make a buck, it's all about them. You know? Their own lives are so important. They don't want or care about community. What would it be like to live in a place where everyone contributed to the betterment of the whole?" she asked.

"Like they have in Europe? Trains and busses, bike trails and subsidized communities," he said.

"I want an urban vibe, where people of all ages come together to be together, to do things together. The Williston mindset is every-person-for-themself," she said.

"We live in a fast-food nation. A country where corporations buy the politicians. Once they own the politicians the laws are crafted to reflect their goals and values; not what's good for the people, or the country, but what's good for them," Jerry said.

"I don't want to live like that anymore," she said.

"Better get a passport. I'm not sure that exists in America," Jerry replied.

~~~

"I have a job interview with Thurber Trucking," Larry said
~~~

"You're shitting me!" replied Wayne. "You're leaving the rig work?"

"I'm wearing out. My body aches every day. I'm eatin' ibuprofen like M&M's. The water trucking is easy money. You've seen how those guys work. They drive around in a warm truck all day, while we're freezing our asses on the rig. You should think about coming with me," Larry said with enthusiasm.

"What I really want to do is start my own business," said Wayne.

"How are you going to do that?" asked Larry. "How you gonna pay your bills? Just drain your savings until it's all gone?"

"No, I'm not going to drain my savings down to nothing. I'm making an action-plan while I'm here – working for the man," Wayne replied.

"See, whenever I'm on the job, working for someone else, my mind always drifts, because I don't really like the job; I'm not interested in it. It's not about the job being *good* or *bad*. It's about me, not being *interested* in the job," Wayne said.

"I've always just taken any job I could find. As long as I can remember. I always took whatever came along. I was happy to be making some money. It was always about money, still is," Wayne continued. "How do you find a job you like? How can you try-out a job that you're not qualified for? That's what kids should be doing in high school. They should have internships at a variety of job-types during their school years. So they can see what's out there. Get an idea in a real-world kind of way, what different jobs are like. Otherwise, it feels like you're just a cog in the capitalist meat-grinder."

"I've only heard people 'talk bad' about socialism. Are you saying the opposite? That socialism is good thing?" Larry asked.

"That depends on your world view and your outlook on life. If you want to live in a dog-eat-dog society then you live in the perfect county – the United States. If you have the world view that governments should provide benefits to the citizens, like free education, mass transit, protection of the earth, then Europe is the place to live. They believe in that sort of thing and they have arranged their governments in such a way, that they are able to manifest those philosophies into existence," Wayne continued.

"Do you remember that Animals song? The one goes *'it's a hard world, to get a break in, all the good things, have been taken.'* They had it figured out in the Sixties. The good things *have* been taken. The one-percenters have accumulated all the wealth. They own everything. Their hedge funds are buying up all the apartment buildings, all the foreclosed homes in the country. One day, all the rents paid by tenants will go directly to the one-percenters," Wayne finished.

"Are you a supporter of socialized healthcare too?" Larry asked.

"Sure why not? What's not to like about government sponsored health care? Do you know how much money a typical healthcare CEO made last year?"

Larry shook his head.

"Five million, that's the low average. The United Healthcare CEO took home twelve million," Wayne said. "But it goes a lot further than just healthcare. For instance, did you know that in South Korea they have internet fiber to the home? The same with Japan and the Emirates. They have fast-fiber to the home because their governments want their people to be early adopters of e-commerce, e-learning, e-health, things like that."

"Why doesn't the U.S. have fiber to the home?" asked Larry.

"Good question." Wayne replied. "Could be they're spending the tax revenue building weapons for battles in the Mideast. Could be it's not a national priority. Could be the lobbyists for the telcos are preventing the build-out. You follow the money; you'll always get your answer."

Wayne sighed and tried to relax. He realized he was getting worked up.

"You're right about being constantly sore. But I like the rig work. Don't know if I could sit in a truck day after day. How you gonna play the interview?" Wayne asked.

"Hmmm, like any job interview. Just put on my happy face, act interested, hope they give me the job," Larry replied.

"Wrong," said Wayne.

"Most people walk into a job interview with hat-in-hand, doing their best to show interest, if not excitement at the possibility of working for the employer. They want to appear as *pleasers.* The job seeker *thinks* they are doing the right thing, and knocking it out of the park. They themselves don't really think that way in real life, but they want to give the impression that they do," Wayne stated.

"When in fact, they don't!" Larry replied.

"Exactly," said Wayne. "The better way for the interviewee to conduct themselves, is to act disinterested. Not disdain just a casual, nonchalant *I could care less demeanor*," said Wayne.

"Do you know how the employer views each candidate?" Wayne asked.

Larry shook his head.

"The 'pleaser' candidate doesn't bring anything to the table. Employers can see that right away. The last thing they want is a non-motivated, 'pretender' employee who acts like they care, but they really don't care," Wayne chortled.

"Now the second candidate brings something to the table – *a keen eye and attitude.* The guy or gal sees the job for what it is – and it ain't enough to get excited about. The employer, seeing the *it ain't enough attitude,* wants the person even more, because the employer knows, the candidate is right, *the job has no wow factor.* It *ain't* enough. The candidate has some panache," Wayne continued.

Larry nodded his head. He loved it when Wayne got on a roll like this.

"The same goes for money," Wayne continued.

"Candidate one – the pleaser; they will take anything.

The first low-ball offer that comes their way they accept. However, candidate two – the disinterested, will *not* take the first, nor the second offer – *because they don't really want the job.* But the employer, who's greedy and always looking to save money, insults candidate number two with low-ball offers. That's the corporate playbook, what else can they do? They can't offer 'em top dollar right out of the gate," Wayne said.

"So candidate two blows them off immediately. They don't respond to phone calls or emails. They just go dark. So the employer tries again. They offer to pay *more* than the mid-point of the salary range which they believe is *more than* fair, as it's higher than mid-point and more than other people are getting," said Wayne.

"Well, that doesn't work either. Candidate number two immediately walks away from it. Now the employer is concerned. Faced with losing the worker *they really want*, they're left with only one option – offer top dollar," Wayne said smiling.

"After the top-dollar offer is received, candidate number two is willing to talk. Negotiations can finally begin. Both parties have achieved their goal. Employer gets the candidate they want; Candidate gets maximum salary in exchange for giving up their current status. A true *quid quo pro* transaction," Wayne said, ending his soliloquy.

"That's an interesting way of looking at it. Do you think I should try that today, for the truck driving job?" asked Larry.

"Fuck no. I'd take whatever they offer you," laughed Wayne.

~~~

The dead of winter. That's what people call it. So cold that nothing moves. Nothing can move. Snow and ice solidify everything in place; anything movable is locked solid to the ground – even the fierce winds can't move things around.

Jerry rode along with Marky-Mark, on their way to a rig accident with a fatality. Death was commonplace in Williston. Numerous car accidents; mostly booze-fueled rollovers that ejected passengers into the snow, where their bodies lay broken from impact or dead from freezing in a North Dakota ditch.

Mark's face was showing the stress of the continuous police activity. Day after day, incident after incident; it was taking a toll. His face was taut and his eyes were vacant. But he kept doing his job, day after day, on the freezing, thankless prairie.

"Hey Mark, how long are you going to keep doing this?" Jerry asked.

"Doing what?" Mark responded.

"Doing this non-stop cop work in Williston. There must be easier police work out there," Jerry stated.

"What makes you say that? I like the action. A cop's life should be full of action. Otherwise, what's the point," Mark retorted.
~~~

"Well, I'm just saying – the intensity out here. It never lets up. When was the last time you went on vacation?

Mark said nothing, as he thought about it.

"Fuck if I know. Can't remember going on vacation. Had a few days off now and then, but never went anywhere," Mark said.

"If you could live anywhere in the country. Put your finger on a map and say 'here.' Where would that be?" asked Jerry.

"I guess if I could go anywhere it would be Bozeman, Montana. I was there after I finished college, before I got this job. I went fishing and four-wheeling out there. It's beautiful. I'd go there in a heartbeat. I tried to get a job there, after I finished school, but they weren't hiring," Mark said.

"Maybe you should take some time off. Like a long weekend. Fly out there, walk into the PD and see if they have any openings. You're a highly experienced officer now. Hell, Bozeman's a resort town compared to Williston," Jerry stated.

Mark looked over at him and nodded his head.

"That's not a bad idea. I've got a ton of PTO built up. Maybe go out there to ski for a couple days."

"Maybe get laid while you're there too," Jerry laughed.

"Yeah, maybe your stripper roommate can hook me up with someone," he laughed.

"I'll ask her. She knows girls from all over the

country. They work the circuits so they have big Facebook networks," Jerry said.

"You're serious?" Mark asked incredulously.

"Yeah I'm serious. These gals are highly organized and networked. If she's got a friend out there, you could have a gal waiting for you. Might cost you some money, but hell, you got lots of money," Jerry laughed.

"Ask her," Mark replied.

They pulled into the Rancor Drilling rig site. Men in blue jumpsuits wearing heavy coats were milling around smoking cigarettes. Work had stopped on account of the accident.

Mark approached the men while Jerry snapped a few photos.

"Tell me about it," Mark asked the rig manager.

"Well, Kenny rode the rig-line up to the top, which is normal practice. He was up there fixing some cabling and musta slipped," said the rig man.

"Was he dead when he hit the platform then?" Mark asked.

"Sir, that's an eighty foot drop onto a solid steel platform. He was dead the moment he hit it. He never made a sound or had any heartbeat, because we checked him. I think his neck is busted," said the rig manager.

"It's a fast way to go. Otherwise if your neck don't

bust, your internal organs are all ruptured and that's a painful way to die. I seen it happen before. Kenny didn't feel nothing."

"We're glad you're here. We can't work until this is resolved and its unsettling for the men to see him there. So as soon as you're done we can get back to work," the rig manager said.

"Well I'm sure your company will understand a little work slow-down on account of this. The death of a worker is no small thing. I'm surprised OSHA isn't out here to shut you down for a week while they investigate," Mark retorted, a bit pissed off.

"Yeah, well the company called me on the cell phone and says to keep the crew out here and get back to work as soon as the body is removed. I'm just following orders," replied the rig manager.

"How old was Kenny," ask Mark.

"Kenny was only twenty-two. He come up here from Vernal, Utah to work. He was a good guy and good worker. It's too bad this happened," said the rig manager.

"Only twenty-two. His life is over before it began. Probably just moved out of the house. Living on his own, making his way through life for the first time. Then a slip off the icy steel and it's all over," Mark lamented. "Now the county sheriff has to notify his family in Utah."

"I'm sorry about all that. This is dangerous work. Everybody knows that," said the rig manager.

"Yup, and men keep coming up here to make money,

regardless of the danger, regardless of their ability," said Mark.

The ambulance arrived and they carted off Kenny's body. The other rig workers milled about, not saying much, knowing they could have been on the gurney, instead of Kenny.

Marky and Jerry got back in the squad car and headed back to town. Neither man said anything as they each starred out the car windows, alone with their thoughts. Death has a way of doing that; sends people several levels deep.

The squad car radio squelched and blurted out.

"We have a train-vehicle accident on 54th street. Any units available to respond please advise."

Mark picked up the mic, "This is forty-two, I am en route. ETA about ten minutes."

"How the fuck do people get hit by trains?" Marky yelled.

They arrived at the rural intersection. A Peterbilt dump truck lay smashed in the ditch. The Burlington Northern Santa Fe freight train with three SD40 engines idled on the tracks. The head locomotive suffered significant damage to the front end.

Mark and Jerry ran to the truck. Mark opened the door and spoke to the driver, who was alive and conscious, but bleeding like a zombie from his head and face.

"My ribs are busted and my neck is fucked up," the

trucker groaned in serious pain.

"You're going to need a few Advil, fella," Mark blurted out as he turned to Jerry.

"We're not going to move him. We'll wait for the medics to get a collar on his neck," Mark said. "I gotta go talk to the engineer of the train and hear what the fuck happened."

The engineer was waiting in the warm locomotive cab, not wanting to go outside into the cold until absolutely necessary. He climbed down from the cab when Mark waved for him to come out.

"So we're high-balling out of town with a string of sixty grain cars. Out here, in the middle of nowhere, this dumb-fuck drives across the uncontrolled intersection. I couldn't even apply the brakes; it happened that fast. I don't think the jackass even looked. He just came across. Lucky for him, we were only going about thirty; if we'd had some speed up we coulda split him in two. I've had it happen a couple times already. I've been railroading for twenty-three years and it never ceases to amaze me how stupid people are," the white bearded engineer barked.

"Now this truck driver, he wasn't trying to beat the train, I'll give him that. He's just an inattentive driver. His inattention almost cost him his life," growled the surly engineer. "Now I gotta sit here all day. The FRA is gonna interrogate me, I'll have to piss in the bottle and I may even get suspended on account of this," he fumed.

"Thanks for your statement Casey. You can go warm your ass in the engine now," Mark scoffed as he turned away.

Another day, the Williston Way.

~~~

The Dakota Gas propane truck pulled into Elmer Hayes' driveway. The propane tank for the home was located at the rear area of the house, near the field. The moment the driver got out of the cab – he could smell it – the stink of septic waste. The driver winced his nose and pulled the fuel-hose across the snow to the storage tank. It wasn't the first time he had smelled stench from a barnyard.

Foo-ya, something stinks like shit.

He connected the hose to the six-hundred gallon tank and began filling it up. As the propane pump buzzed in the cold air, the driver walked inside the tire tracks left in the snow to the edge of a field. He stopped and held his breath; the field was covered with human feces, toilet paper, and reeked to high-heaven. This wasn't barnyard manure, this was human shit illegally dumped.

Old Elmer is making some side-money.

The driver didn't like Elmer. The old fart was a prick and always rubbed him the wrong way. The health department was going to get a call on this.

Two days later North Dakota Health Department investigator Molly Potaski, arrived at the toxic waste ranch. She knocked on the door, but Elmer wasn't home. The anonymous tipster reported a large amount of human waste dumped behind the property. She pulled her coat tight to her neck for protection from the nasty wind,
~~~

grabbed her sample kit from the truck and walk to the rear of the property. She could smell it in the air - the stench was horrific.

She had seen this type of situation several times before. The oilfield porta-potties were pumped into trucks and the waste was dumped wherever the sewage guys could find a place for it. Sometimes they just opened the valve on the passenger side of the truck and drove down the gravel roads, ejecting waste into the ditches and the roadway. Everyone was making fast-money. The septic guys were no different. The hard part was catching them and fining them.

She circled the dump area, carefully avoiding the dung, taking photos and samples in her plastic test-lab vials. She had driven a long way to get to the site; the sun was out so she wanted to make the most of her trip. As she moved along the perimeter, she noticed another set of tracks in the snow – older tire tracks.

After walking fifty yards, the field opened up into a small ravine. What she saw gave her a fright. Frack sand had been dumped in big piles. This was "hot" sand; she was sure of it. The landowner was using his ranch land as a toxic waste dump. Sewage was one thing; most of the time the health department did nothing, other than threaten fines and lecture the landowners. But radioactive frack-sand was another issue. That would fall under the Federal EPA jurisdiction. They could seize the land, fine the owner or both.

She pulled out her cell phone and made the call.

Two hours later federal investigators were onsite with

hazmat suits and Geiger counters. They confirmed the frack sand was hot. When Elmer pulled in his driveway he was shocked to see cars, trucks, and people in space-suits walking around his property. He walked out to the field and stood among the investigators, pretending he didn't know anything.

A federal investigator barked at him.

"How many times have you allowed radioactive materials dumped on your land," he asked calmly.

Elmer shrugged his shoulders. "I'm not sure how this got here."

"Are you playing dumb or plain dumb?" the Fed asked him, now clearly irritated. He wasn't going to take any of the *dumb-farmer act.* He knew from past experience that farmers pretended to be illiterate know-nothings – when it was convenient for them. In reality they were sneaky manipulators who worked every government program for free-money "subsidies." These "poor honest farmers" sucked more money from the government teat than all the welfare queens put together.

"I don't know how this got on my property," Elmer said again.

"Well if that's the case then I will ask the federal judge to seize this entire property as a hazardous waste site. We have the power to do that you know. Ever since the methamphetamine cook-houses came into existence. The government will seize this entire property, including your home. You'll lose it all with no compensation."

Elmer's mouth fell open.

"That's right, Mr. Green Jeans, why don't you think about for bit, get the wax out of your ears and your priorities straight; then I'm going to ask you once more. I'm going to need names if you want to hang on to your property," the Federal agent scolded. "In addition to the radioactive sand, you have about a half-million gallons of human waste illegally dumped out here. I hope you have a good lawyer."

Elmer was stunned. He had never seen this coming. He was going to have to roll over and give up the name of the oil company guy.

~~~

Jerry walked into the Williston library to attend a so-called "community roundtable." In reality, the meeting was an opportunity for a bought-n-sold Republican senator to stump for the Keystone XL pipeline. There wasn't going to be any discourse between the bureaucrat and citizens.

The town big-wigs were all there, back-slapping and brown-nosing each other, trying to get chummy and ingratiate themselves with the VIP. They pretended to be one big, happy-family. There were a family of sorts– they were 'the haves.' The 'have-nots' were on the other end of town.

Jerry counted Mayor Fitzgerald, all the city council members and some county officials. Jerry noticed the Mayor was dressing more upscale of late. His hunyunk appearance of plaid shirts had been replaced with white-starched shirts, no tie and upscale sport jackets. He was starting to dress like a millionaire. Jerry looked at the Mayor's feet, half expecting to see deck-shoes for a yacht.
~~~

Fitzgerald was wearing Ferragamo.

He didn't buy those in town.

The Republican stepped to the podium, surrounded by full-color placards with maps and graphs of the proposed Keystone oil pipeline project. He spoke on and on about the benefits of the pipeline, and how the Republicans had attempted to sneak it through the legislative session by attaching it to a highway bill called the Moving Ahead For Progress in the 21st Century. They hoped to bypass the President by bundling it, but unfortunately for them, it was torpedoed in the Senate.

Everyone knew the "billionaire brothers" were behind the project. The "Coke-Brothers" as people referred to them, owned significant assets in the US and Canada, they funded politicians with monster donations, they bought stooges in the media, and funded private "think tanks."

No matter how hard they tried, the pipeline couldn't get any traction in Congress. The reason was simple – there was another big player in the game – a player who didn't want the pipeline. Their opposition was also a billionaire, a shrewd old-geezer who looked like grandpa and one of the richest men in the world. He owned the railroad that transported the frack stand from Wisconsin to the Dakotas, and the oil out of the Bakken Range. The Keystone pipeline would undermine his monopoly; so he used his significant political influence and money, to derail the pipeline project when it came to a hearing or a vote in Congress.

"The building and operation of Keystone will have no effect on global carbon emissions," said the politician.

"These are shovel-ready jobs for hard-working Americans. The Yellow Tractor Company will benefit greatly. They have manufacturing plants all over America employing thousands of workers."

He looked down at his notes and continued to read his prepared comments.

"With high gas prices and high unemployment in the country, this project should be a top priority for Congress and the Administration. It is crucial to our national security."

"The pipeline is already being built. Enbridge has begun construction of the Flanagan South Pipeline which will connect Chicago to Cushing, Oklahoma. This pipeline does not cross the international border and needs no presidential approval. It is time for us to put this environmentalist hysteria to bed and approve this pipeline which is clearly in the national interest."

As Jerry wrote in his notebook, the guy next to him grew agitated.

"This guy's so full of shit it makes me want to puke," he said to Jerry.

"We need Otoya Yamaguchi in this room, right now," the guy said, seething with anger.

"Who is that? The Yamaguchi guy? Is that Kristi's brother?" asked Jerry.

"Yamaguchi was a 17-year old Japanese radical who used a sword to assassinate Inejiro Asanuma in 1960. Asanuma was a political-traitor – just like this guy," he continued.

"We live in the Age of Cowardice. It's disgusting. Look at that crook Bernie Madoff. There wasn't anyone, including the victims of his Ponzi scheme, that had enough courage to take a magnum pistol and shoot holes in his chest. Hell, they could pay a prison guard or a convict to kill him in prison. It's all about sending a message. In the Sixties, politicians were always at risk of getting assassinated. Today, a bullshit artist like this guy can stand up here with impunity and talk shit without anyone coming at him."

Jerry nodded his head up and down.

"You certainly have a point. It's been a while since a U.S. politician was killed," Jerry said.

"The country's gone to hell," the extremist guy said, as he got up and left his chair.

Jerry flipped his notebook closed and left the room. He had listened to enough bullshit for one night and he needed a drink. He decided to stop in the Queen of Hearts and watch Lisa work the pole.

~~~

The strip-club was dark and seedy. A five-dollar cover charge to get in – followed by six-dollar bottles of beer. He stood next to the bar and watched as the men whooped and hollered at the dancer, a black girl of about twenty-two. She had a nice body, strong legs and killer abs.

"How ya doing" said the roughneck standing next to him.
~~~

"I'm all right how about you," responded Jerry, not really interested in striking up a conversation.

"I'm glad to be in town for the night. I have three days off and I need to get drunk and get laid," said the roughneck.

"The getting drunk part will be easy, not sure about getting laid," replied Jerry.

"I'm hoping this nigger doesn't dance all night," said the roughneck.

"You don't like her?" asked Jerry.

"Well, I don't know her personally but don't really care for black people all that much," he replied.

"Do you like her?" asked the oil-bigot.

"Yeah, I like her. What's not to like?" Jerry replied.

"Well, true," replied the bigot, slobbering a bit as he belched up beer bubble. "I just want to watch white women tonight."

"I can tell you this pal," Jerry said. "I've been fucked-over worse by white people, than black people."

"Me too," said the roughneck. "Now that I think about it."

Jerry realized the guy was drunk and he needed to get away from him, but there was nowhere else to stand.

The music stopped and the black girl left the stage and hopped on a lap for a twenty dollar bill.

Shouting and whistling erupted as Lisa came out of the dressing room wearing nothing but a G-string and a black leather police hat and vest.

An oldie from the Fine Young Cannibals blasted from the jukebox; Lisa went into her routine.

She drives me crazy, I can't help myself.

She drives me crazy, I can't help myself.

She was erotic, sensuous and playful – all in the same routine. The men dropped tens, twenties, fifties, around the stage hoping to coax her to come their way; see her titties up close.

No wonder she was here. She was so natural at this – it wasn't even work.

The hard part was living in Williston, not the dancing. The boredom, the cold, the bleak landscape of semi-trucks, oil wells and pipe. This was not a place to live; it was a place to work.

Lisa was right. Portland was sounding better and better.

~~~

Fitzgerald's Hardware moved into the new Lind building in March. The towns-people were surprised by the news at first, but then, after a week, not so much. Everything was changing around town. The hardware store moving from the center of town was no big deal. The Mayor was pleased that no one even questioned the fact that the building had been approved by him; either that or they didn't care. People were too busy making money to care about little things like cronyism and backdoor deals.

The old hardware store site was quickly occupied by Todd Lundquist, a tattoo artist. The obese townie had once been a sharp-shooting point guard for the high school basketball team. Since then his body had grown to more than three hundred pounds and his goatee measured ten inches. When people asked him why he grew his goatee so long, he told them he wanted to keep it the same length as his cock. Not that anyone would know. He was a bible-thumping Christian, married, with three kids. His shop was called *316 Creations* and he specialized in religious crosses, fish symbols and bible passages in cursive.

The Mayor walked into his old building to have a look-see at the new tenant and how he was doing – and
~~~

probe if there was a way to extort some money from Todd. He knew Todd had come into a sizeable inheritance after his father was killed in a combine accident. His poor old man had his arms ripped off by a malfunctioning power-take-off shaft. A money-grubbing trial lawyer had rushed in and extracted a half-million dollars from the manufacturer's insurance company – that went into a trust fund for Todd.

Knowing he wouldn't have to go to college and didn't have to farm, Todd drifted in life from the age of eighteen – first gold mining in Alaska, and then building his own airfield on the family ranch outside of Williston. The airfield was his best idea, as the private companies not only paid to use his runway but also store their planes in his hangers. All of which was outside of the Williston city limits, beyond the reach of Fitzgerald.

"Hi Todd," the Mayor said as he walked into the tattoo parlor.

"Well Mayor Fitzgerald, what brings you here?" he asked, knowing full-well the asshole wasn't there for a tattoo.

Play it cool – see what the Mayor wanted.

"I suppose you're looking for a tattoo that says Mayor, huh?" Todd laughed.

"No Todd, I'm not interested in a tattoo. Tattoos are for sailors, Marines, and this new generation. They like the ink-work and piercings," Fitzgerald countered.

"How's business? What kind of work are you getting?" Fitzgerald asked.

“Well you know the typical work. Women like to get flowers and hearts, birds and vines. The men from the oil fields get derricks and pumping stations. I had a dumb-ass from Wisconsin ask me to put a Green Bay Packer helmet on his back, but I refused. I had to draw a line on that. I’ll do band names and logos, Harley-Davidson of course, but not corporations or sports teams,” he said.

“I didn’t know that morality was involved with a tattoo business,” said the Mayor. “I figure that money is money; you provide what they ask for.”

“No, not exactly. See the difference is; I’m an artist. I don’t just do any request that comes in the door. There may be people that do that, but I’m not one of them. But I appreciate you asking,” Todd stated.

“Another reason I came in here was to ask you about getting a permit,” Fitzgerald said.

Todd nodded his head. He knew something like this was coming.

“I don’t need a permit to operate my business. The state has no requirements for a permit and neither does Williston. I checked all that out before I started this business,” Todd replied.

“Well, just because you didn’t need a permit to open your shop, doesn’t mean you don’t need a permit to continue doing business in Williston,” the Mayor countered.

“For instance, take the street vendors. They used to come into Williston and park on the street and sell their hot food to workers – without a permit. It was all perfectly legal as long as their kitchen areas had passed health department inspections."

"I don't sell food and I'm not in a food wagon," Todd said.

"Yes, but the point is, the Williston city council passed an ordinance *requiring* food vendors have a permit to operate in town. The same thing could happen with your tattoo shop," the Mayor said, grinning at Todd.

"Oh I see what you're saying now," Todd answered. "You're going to force me to get a permit, after the fact, because my business is successful and you want a piece of the action. You're starting to run Williston like Las Vegas."

"Well not me personally, Todd. The permit fee goes to the city for upkeep and maintenance, salaries, things like that," Fitzgerald said.

"Is there some way that you and I could avoid this permit thing?" asked Todd, wanting to see if the Mayor was willing to extort him for personal gain.

"Well, there are many ways to conduct business and get things done. If you know the right people," Fitzgerald replied. "Why don't you think it over? We'll have a strategy session and see if we can avoid this whole permit thing," Fitzgerald said, as he laid his business card on the counter.

Fitzgerald looked around at the walls and the various pictures and photos of recent tattoos.

"Some of these are interesting, but they're a bit too Goth for my tastes," he said as he left the building.

Todd glared at him as he left the store. He was angry, but he had a plan.

We'll have a strategy session, that's for sure.

CHAPTER V

The snow melted and spring was upon the prairie. The long, dark winter was over and people felt a sense of relief, like a hurricane had passed over and they had survived. They crept out of their houses and trailers with pale-white skin, looking around cautiously, as if a *Walking Dead* zombie might be nearby. Winter coats were abandoned as townfolks took in the sunshine.

The street sweeper cleared the pea gravel from the dirty streets, as the trees and bushes began to bud out. The first Saturday in May the grubby-looking fisherman stood along the banks of the Missouri River; whipping treble-hooks into the river, hoping to snag a giant paddlefish.

For the Mayor, it was another year of the building boom; another opportunity to make more money and finalize his exit strategy for Vegas. He met Ken Hotchkiss, a local realtor, at the Wooden Shoe restaurant.

"You're really selling out?" asked the realtor. "Things are still picking up; there's a lot of money to be made around here."

"I'm getting tired of the hardware store business. The Mayor-job is taking more and more of my time and I just don't have the desire to work that hard. Going in at night to do the books and reorder merchandise; it's a headache. Now's a good time for me to sell the business," Fitzgerald said.

"I suppose you're right. Before too long they might

get a Menards or Home Depot out here and that would be bad for your business," the realtor said.

Fitzgerald feigned agreement by nodding his head.

The dumb-fuck has no idea that I control what businesses can come to town.

"Yes, good point. I need to sell out before a big company like that muscles-in on me," he lied.

"So anyway, I want to list my house too. I don't need a big house like that. Just get me the market price. I'm not looking for a big number," Fitzgerald said.

"Alrighty then, I'll get the paperwork for both places over to you this week and we'll put 'em on the market. Thanks for listing with me," Hotchkiss said.

"Sure sure. We go back a long time. But I tell you what; there's a lot of folks out here now that I don't even know who they are. Just strangers to me," Fitzgerald said.

"I see that every day. People walking in, right off the street; acting like they'd known me forever," Hotchkiss said. "But I tell 'em, there ain't enough houses to go around. But that's going to change soon I hear."

"Why's that?" asked Fitzgerald.

"That big Colorado building company is coming up here to build a thousand-unit apartment complex. Right out there by the airport. They bought the old Orville Boone property. He made a fortune on it. A hundred acres for five-thousand an acre; that's five hundred thousand –

just like that. That'll keep that old coot in fish-fry's and bingo for the rest of his days," laughed Hotchkiss.

"I wasn't aware of that transaction, that's complete news to me. But it's good news, Williston needs more housing," Fitzgerald rambled.

How the fuck did that happen without me knowing about it?

~~~

Fitzgerald walked to the Planning and Zoning department for a chat with Harold Bloom. The place was crazy-busy with customers and the staff was swamped. After waiting around for a half hour, Bloom got free.

"How can I help you Mayor?" asked Bloom.

"I'm curious about the parcel that Orville Boone sold. What can you tell me about that transaction?" Fitzgerald asked.

"Well, a developer out of Colorado purchased the land with the intention of building a mega apartment complex on the property. It's already zoned for that type of building so there's no issue with P&Z. Is this the first you've heard about it? Cybak has been heavily involved in the process. I'm surprised you aren't in the loop," Bloom responded.

"Me too," said Fitzgerald. "Thanks."

Cybak is out-hustling me for cash!

Fitzgerald left the zoning office and walked to the
~~~

post office where Cybak worked as a clerk. He had some letters to mail anyway so it was a good opportunity to ping Cybak.

He waited in line and noticed all the transients were getting postal money orders so they could send their paychecks home.

Times are tough. The rest of the country is in recession from the mortgage-fraud collapse of 2008, but Williston is booming.

When it was his turn he stepped up to the counter.

"Mr. Cybak, do you have time for lunch today? I'll treat you to lunch at Subway," Fitzgerald offered.

"Sure, I'm always looking for a free meal. See you there at noon," Cybak said.

Fitzgerald had an hour to kill so walked over to the liquor store to pick up some beer. The price of a six-pack shocked him.

Twelve dollars for a 6-pack of beer. That's two-bucks-a-bottle.

He grabbed a double-IPA craft-brew and walked to the counter.

"Holy Cow," Fitzgerald said to the clerk, pretending to have sticker-shock. "Don't know if I can afford a six-pack at this price," he mused.

"The cost of living is high these days," said the high-on-pot clerk. "You wanna play you gotta pay."

"I like that," said Fitzgerald. "I'm going to start using that one when people complain about the high cost of goods and services around here."

"Enjoy," the stoner said as he handed him his change.

Fitzgerald went to his car with the beer and rummaged through his glove box for the bottle opener.

These fucking microbrews don't use twist-off's.

"Where in the fuck is my church-key?" he said, as he pulled out various junk from his glove box. He found his opener at the very bottom, underneath his insurance cards, GPS, radar detector, and cheese knife. He tilted his seat back and took a couple long swigs of the beer. A nice spring day, sun was shining; he needed to put the squeeze on Cybak.

That fucker is gaming me.

He could see the post office from where he was parked and after his second beer, Cybak left the building and started walking towards Subway. Fitzgerald met him at the doorway and purchased a $15 dollar sub for each of them. They slid into a corner booth.

"You fucking dink," Fitzgerald said, looking him in the eye.

Cybak looked over his shoulder. "Are you talking to me?" he asked.

"You been working a deal under the table with a Colorado developer on the Boone property," Fitzgerald said. "Don't play stupid with me. When were you going to pull me in on the deal? Were you going to wait until the whole council heard about it?"

"Don't get your undies in a bunch. I was going to include you as soon as I got the suitcases worked out," Cybak said.

"Oh yeah?" said a skeptical Fitzgerald. "Just like the adult bookstore permit you rammed through at the last council meeting? When do I get paid for that one? You're a couple payments behind, buddy."

"Listen, you never bring me in on your deals until it's show time. This is no different," Cybak argued.

"Okay, guess I have to trust you on this. If you need any help you let me know. An apartment complex of this magnitude – we should be working out the details together. I'd hate to see you sell-low, if you catch my drift," Fitzgerald said.

"I'll let you know if I need your help. You work your side of the fence and I'll work mine. There's enough for everybody. Plenty to go around, you know that," said Cybak. "Thanks for the sub, I gotta get back to work," he said, as he stood up to leave.

"Nice seeing ya," Fitzgerald said back.

I have to watch you like a hawk.

~~~

"You spent $650,000 building three toilets?" Jerry asked.
~~~

"Well, yeah," said Darin Lockhart the Williston Parks and Recreation Director. "The old park toilets were old and crappy," he said, trying to be funny.

"I'm not saying they shouldn't have been replaced," said Jerry, "but six-fifty divided by three is $216,000 per toilet. The sewer and water was already stubbed in."

"We had the money from the one-cent sales tax that voters approved last year," Lockhart said.

Lockhart was dodging the question. Jerry kept shaking his head.

"I wasn't asking you where the money came from," Jerry said. "I'm questioning the hefty expenditure."

Lockhart said nothing and just looked away.

"Who got the contract for building these toilets?" Jerry asked.

"I'd have to look in the RFP," Lockhart lied, "I don't remember off the top of my head."

"Okay then, thanks for your time," Jerry said as he left the Parks office.

The fix was in; Lockhart was getting a huge kickback.

His next stop was the Williston Fire Department. Chief Johnson had requested a huge budget increase; Jerry needed the details for an article on the upcoming budget.

The double-chinned Chief took Jerry into his office. Jerry noticed the Chief was so fat, he barely fit in his chair.

"We are overwhelmed with calls. I have ten full-time crew members and I need at least sixteen to run the operation right," said the Chief. "We need the extra men due to the increase in the city's population and the number of calls coming in."

"Are the current firefighters full-time or volunteer?" asked Jerry.

"They're all volunteer," said the Chief.

"So if you add fifty percent more volunteers, where does the $400,000 that you're requesting go?" Jerry asked.

"That's for equipment and insurance costs," the Chief retorted.

"What kind of equipment are you needing?" Jerry asked.

"Mainly replacement of worn-out equipment, updates to some of our gear," the Chief replied with straight-face.

Jerry could smell the graft. The Fire Chief was working a kick-back, just like the Parks Director.

"How is the city council viewing your request? Is there money available from the one-cent sales tax?" Jerry asked.

"The Williston Fire Department is not able to use the sales-tax proceeds, so the council will have to allocate the money from the normal budget," the Chief explained. "So far they've been receptive. The budget request is under advisement and up for discussion at the next meeting."

Jerry forced a smile – *he smelled a rat.*

He had seen enough of their dealings to know some of them were getting kick-backs for these projects. The Mayor was; probably a few others too.

~~~

Wayne had a five-day vacation from the drilling rigs. The long, nasty winter was over and he was tempted to go fishing – like the other guys. But that would mean buying a cheap rod-n-reel from Walmart, plus he'd need some hooks and weights, and a license; he decided against it.

He was intrigued by the huge "Oil Show Conference" going on in Williston. With free admission and dozens of trade show booths, there was potential of a non-rig job opportunity. He cleaned up and took the shuttle from his man camp into town.

The woman who ran the Oil-Line Shuttle was a grouchy prairie gal named Carol Paulaha. She was on the wrong-side of forty and fading fast.

"How's it going?" Wayne asked her.

"Oh fine I guess. As long as I don't have to deal with the city council," she said.

"They giving you trouble?" Wayne asked.

"Oh yeah. Those fuckers, pardon my French, they won't let me operate within the city limits of Williston unless I get a taxi permit. They won't give me a taxi
~~~

permit unless I apply for the permit, which is $300 bucks. That's just to apply; don't mean they'll give me the permit," she said.

"That sucks." Wayne replied. "You'd think they'd want taxi service; keep drunks from driving."

"You'd think. But they just want money for every freaking permit," she vented. "I still give rides around Williston, but I can't charge, I can only take tips. These man camp trips is where I make my money."

She continued talking the entire drive into Williston. Wayne added a few comments, but he wanted to stay quiet and look out the window. Carol made that impossible with her chatter. When they finally arrived in town he said "so long," gave her a $5 tip, and got off the shuttle.

The Grand Hotel displayed a large, oil-black banner with gold letters BAKKEN GOLD from the entrance. Wayne went inside and walked around the perimeter of the conference center, listening, watching, getting the lay-of-the-land inside the large room. More than three hundred people milled about, mostly carpet-baggers from out of state, trying to sell their services.

A man keyed up a microphone to talk.

"Ladies and gentlemen, I'm pleased to introduce our keynote speaker today. He's the CEO of Continental Oil and a businessman most of you know by his pro-drilling reputation. Please give a round of applause for Henry Hamm," he stated.

A plump, mid-60's man with too much size and girth walked to the podium. Wayne noticed the billionaire was wearing a cheap suit, probably from J.C. Penny's.

"Energy production is now and always has been an integral part of the American economy. Petroleum production is the safety net for this country's economy. It ensures our national security and it is a means of wealth creation in America. Many things flow from American oil," he assured the audience.

"But we have problems that threaten our future production," he paused for dramatic effect.

"The future of the Williston oil play as well as other basins is dependent upon removing President Obama from office. His policy is a total failure. His policy is based on scarcity. That's a thing of the past. He believed we were running out of oil. That belief funneled resources into alternatives that are not practical," Hamm stated.

"We know and geologists have confirmed that the Williston basin is a super-sized deposit. Enough to last decades. My company is planning on investing more resources, more technology to make these wells more efficient and more productive, in order to benefit the economic development of states like North Dakota," he continued.

"I'm also happy to announce, if you haven't already heard the news, that North Dakota has just surpassed Alaska in oil production. It is now the second highest oil producing state in the nation," he yelled. "North Dakota oil is getting the world's attention. We need to start operating as a world-class oil producer. We need a major pipeline here. I don't support just the Keystone pipeline, I support all of them. We need all we can get!"

The audience came to their feet with applause.

Wayne had seen and heard enough. Hamm was preaching to the choir. Everyone in the room was there to make money off the 'oil play' so it was one big feel-good and blow-me convention. He got up from his chair and walked to the exit. As he exited the building he noticed a nice-looking 30-something woman with a small green sign that read – GAAF, Green Americans Against Fracking.

"What is this about?" he asked her.

"I represent GAAF, we're an anti-fracking group," she said. "We're looking for support from people who are against fracking, not only because of the pollution aspect but also to reduce the carbon footprint of humans. Just because there's oil available deep in the ground, that doesn't mean we should stop the green initiatives that are underway," she said.

"I couldn't agree more. We already have significant wind-farms and solar panels are everywhere, even on the drilling rigs," he said.

"Really," she said. "On the rigs? Do you work on the rigs?" she asked.

"Yes, I work for Continental. They install solar panels on their remote stations to power sensors and SCADA devices," Wayne replied. "There's no electricity out there in the middle of the prairie."

"What did you think of the Bakken Gold presentation?" she asked.

"I think Hamm is full of shit and full of himself. I guess when you're worth twelve billion dollars, you get a bit of ego and the hubris goes along with it," Wayne said. "They announced that North Dakota has one-hundred forty millionaires now. Some of the people are getting rich beyond their dreams. Most are just earning a living, and suffering to do that."

"Let me ask you something," Wayne said. "Are you a volunteer or are you paid?"

"I'm a paid attorney. We're all paid. GAAF is funded by several wealthy dot-com entrepreneurs and donations from the public," she said. "My name is Amber McKendrick," she said, holding out her hand.

"You're an attorney?" Wayne asked, a bit surprised, as he shook her hand.

"Yes, I am. I graduated from University of Montana, in Missoula," she said.

"How long do you have to stand post here?" Wayne asked. "Do you want to have dinner with me?"

"I'm here for another hour, after that, sure. I have no food with me so I'd like to go out to eat."

"Do you eat steak? Wayne asked, "I'm craving a steak from Ma Ringer's Chop House."

"Yes, of course. I'm on a paleo-diet. I don't eat carbs. You can eat my bun," she said with wink.

Jesus Christ, she just winked at me.

"Okay, I'll see you over there in an hour. I'll get us

a table. Otherwise there will be a long wait once these yahoos leave Hamm's school-of-oil seminar," he said.

"See you in an hour," she said.

~~~

"We are hiring if you're interested," Amber said, as she cut into her steak.

"Actually, I am interested. There are a lot of shady things happening at these rigs. Certainly the pollution aspects," Wayne replied.

"I'm aware of some of that," she said. "Like the cracked well-casings; We litigate on that all the time."

"What about the well-casings? They're solid concrete," Wayne asked quizzically.

"Yes, they are concrete, but, the failure rate of the casing is five-percent the first year! And it goes up every year after that. Once the lining is cracked, underground methane escapes and contaminates the aquifer. Leaving people with undrinkable water. It's happening all over in Pennsylvania. Have you heard of Dimock? It's a township in Pennsylvania. The entire community has no drinking water. The entire aquifer has been polluted by defective fracking. That's happening everywhere. This fracking epidemic is worldwide, not just in the USA. The oil companies are doing this everywhere there are known oil deposits. Only a few countries have banned fracking, but our efforts to educate are making a difference," she said.

"I wasn't aware fracking was world-wide, but I'm not
~~~

surprised. This is anything-goes-land. It's really strange; nobody seems to care, as long as they get something out of it. The almighty petro-dollar rules the day out here," Wayne said.

"People have money out here, but Main Street is in trouble. People who scrimp and save their money are being squeezed like a lemon by the Federal Reserve's zero interest rate policy," Amber said.

"I'm surprised retirees and the AARP lobbyists aren't screaming to high-heaven," she said. "That generation planned their retirements on getting some type of yield on their fixed-assets. Now they are getting nothing. They have to burn through their savings just to live," she continued.

"The Feds promote the theory that giving zero-rate money will enable banks and businesses to expand and hire more people and add to the economy. But it doesn't work that way. The banks simply take the money and arbitrage it. They make money without doing anything in terms of organic growth," she continued.

"If you haven't noticed, the shopping malls in the country are collapsing. The middle-class doesn't have any money. The Feds want inflation instead of deflation but that's not happening because people are broke.

"I see inflation when I buy food," Wayne replied. "Pringles chips have gone up fifty percent. They used to cost a buck – now they're a buck-fifty."

"Yeah, and Paul Newman spaghetti sauce has dropped to the same price as Ragu," Amber countered. "Foodstuff is always back and forth like that. They're always resizing the containers to fool the consumer; give them less product for the same money. But on the scale of a shopping mall, those department store products can't be discounted like that. Well-off people don't purchase enough products to sustain malls; they need the middle and lower class people to shop and blow their money on stuff they don't need."

"Do you follow Wall Street?" Wayne asked.

"Well, kind of. I trade my own portfolio online. There's no way I'm giving some money-manager a quarterly fee to move my money from mutual fund to mutual fund. That's just plain stupid. I can do that myself for five-dollars a trade; make my own mistakes instead of someone else doing it for me. My parents were caught in the dot-com collapse. Their investments were controlled by a so-called financial advisor. It took them years, to get back to even. After watching that, I said *no-way*; I'm not letting someone else control my money," she said.

"You're fortunate to have a nest-egg to move around. Most Americans are living paycheck to paycheck. With the housing collapse, they've kicked the chair out from under the middle-class. Homeowners lost all their equity. Most people are still underwater with their homes – they can't sell for even-money. And what's worse, the younger generations aren't going to buy those homes. They don't have high-paying jobs to afford them; they don't want to pay the taxes and upkeep, even if they could get loans. Plus, they don't trust the economy. They want to rent and I don't blame them. I lost my house to foreclosure. Now my credit is trashed, of course, but it made me rethink home ownership in general," Wayne stated.

"In what way?" Amber asked.

"Well, I always tried to do it the right way, like the media encourages. You know, make extra payments to reduce your principal and length of the loan, remodel your kitchen and bath to make it more sellable, pay your taxes on time to avoid penalties, and the crazy never-ending yard work. After losing my house, all of that seems foolish now," Wayne said.

"That's the American Dream right? Beautiful home in the suburbs, paid off, living on easy street," she laughed.

"Yeah, and here's the weird part. My house was owned by Fannie Mae. They got stuck with all the toxic-waste mortgages the bankers didn't want. Then Fannie and Freddie went toes-up and the government took them over, since they were, after all, 'government sponsored entities.' So my house was owned by the federal government, like millions of other homes in the country. Essentially, the government owns the majority of homes in the country. They kicked people out of their homes, so they could reset their books in a way that squares the circle for the bean counters."

"What do you mean? Explain that to me," she asked.

"Okay, I bought my house for $250,000 and put $50,000 as a down payment. That's twenty-percent down. When I went into default I owed $175,000. When the government bought the house back at the foreclosure auction, their attorney was there with a check for $175,000. So they paid themselves the full amount on what was owed. That makes the accounting look better on the books. Then they turned around and sold my house on the open market for $75,000.

"You're kidding me," she said.

"No not kidding you. They never offered me one nickel reduction to stay in my house, to help me preserve my capital, the $50,000 that I put down, plus the paid down equity. They wouldn't help me weather the storm that Wall Street created. They helped all the banks and counter-parties who were exposed - but not Joe-Sixpack. Nope. They kicked me out and resold the property for a $100,000 less than what I owned. It's all a shell game for those in Washington and New York. They don't care about people. They only care about money. Who has it; who's getting it; how can they get more," Wayne finished.

"Do you want to get a bottle of wine and go back to my hotel room?" Amber asked him, looking him straight in the eye.

The waitress was walking by at that very moment.

"Check please," Wayne said, smiling at Amber.

~~~

Todd Lundquist waited for Mayor Fitzgerald to arrive at the restaurant. He decided that it was best to try and negotiate this tattoo permit – rather than use brute force – which wasn't necessary quite yet.

"Hi Marty," Todd said as he rose from dinner-table booth at Ma Ringer's Chop House.

"Hello Todd," Fitzgerald said as they shook hands.

With the fake friendliness over, they each grabbed a menu to look over the lunch specials.
~~~

"I'll have the Philly-steak sandwich with green peppers," Todd said to the frumpy waitress.

"That sounds good, but I'll have the turkey dinner with the giblet gravy and cranberries," the Mayor said.

"So I've been thinking about my predicament and I wanted to meet with you to see what it will take for me to avoid this whole city council permit thing," Todd said as he stroked his long goatee.

"I think that's the wise approach," Fitzgerald said. "It's the smartest way to do business around here. Just head things off before they become a problem."

"You may have heard about the lady who runs a taxi service in and out of town," Fitzgerald commented.

"Carol Paulaha," Todd interjected.

"Yes, you've heard of her. She had the same situation you have. She was operating a taxi service without a permit. Now there are regulations prohibiting taxi service without a permit. She's fighting city hall on the issue; that's just not smart," Fitzgerald said.

"She didn't need a permit when she started her operation two years ago. I didn't need a permit from the city to open and operate a tattoo shop," Todd reminded the Mayor.

"That is quite true. But the thing is, if you know someone at city hall, like you know me, we can work out an arrangement to avoid that permitting drama before it even begins," said Fitzgerald.

The waitress arrived and set their plates in front of them. Todd took a large bite of his steak sandwich as Fitzgerald dug into his turkey dinner smothered in giblet gravy.

"How's your plate of food Mayor?" asked Todd.

"Delicious. Piping hot, just the way I like it," replied the Mayor.

"Do you know where the term "giblet gravy" comes from?" asked the tattoo artist.

"Haven't got a clue," said the Fitzgerald as he shoveled a heaping fork-full of turkey into his mouth.

"It comes from the French Revolution," Todd revealed.

"No shit?" Fitzgerald replied.

"Let me tell you a little about the French Revolution. A revolution occurs when the citizens of a country are tired of being abused by their rulers. So they rise up and arrest all the leaders and put them in jail."

Fitzgerald looked up at him; not liking the direction this was headed.

"Oftentimes, the citizens are so angry at the leaders, that they decide to execute them rather than keep them in jail," Todd continued.

"Now, about the gravy you're eating," Todd smiled.

"During the French Revolution the citizens decided to kill all the former rulers, so they used a device called a guillotine, which I'm sure, you're familiar with. At the time it was called the Halifax Gibbet.

It was the same wooden device. It had a picnic table bench, where the condemned bureaucrat would lay down on. Their head was placed in-between two pieces of wood that had a groove cut out of it in the center to accommodate their neck. Above this piece was a sharp meat-cleaver that was angled at a forty-five degree incline. This cleaver was in a track so it would slide down, from about twelve feet above the bad-guy's neck. People would gather around and watch – this was great entertainment during the 1750's."

"There must be a point to this history lesson, right?" said Fitzgerald, now angry.

"The executioner would pull a lever and the heavy blade would release, slide down the track, and slice through the neck of the bureaucrat, severing the head from the body," Todd said.

"Now here's where the gravy part comes in. Once the head is removed from the body, the stump of the neck ejects blood and fluid all over the stage area. The Englishmen who were in the crowd watching the Gibbet device work its magic, referred to this ejected fluid as Gibbet Gravy, and over the course of a couple hundred years, the pronunciation changed to Giblet Gravy."

"So, that wonderful brown gravy you're eating, flavored with chunks of neck meat, the liver, gizzard and heart; is really a throwback to the French Revolution."

Fitzgerald put down his folk and knife on top of his half eaten lunch.

"The more things change, the more they stay the same," Todd said, looking Fitzgerald in the eyes.

"Do we have an understanding Mr. Mayor?" asked Todd.

Fitzgerald had a blank look on his face; the color had drained from his skin.

"If I hear anything at all about regulations for a tattoo parlor in Williston, I'm going to find you some night, and gut you out like a hog."

"I hope we're clear on this," Todd said, looking straight at Fitzgerald. "I worked on my daddy's hog farm. I've gutted out hundreds of hogs. I know exactly how to do it."

Todd paused for a moment.

"You have nothing to worry about, because you're going to make sure that tattoo parlor regulations never come into existence in Williston. In fact, it's going to give me peace of mind, knowing the Mayor has my back."

The frazzled waitress stopped at their table.

"How's everything tasting?" she asked.

Fitzgerald was speechless, so Todd spoke up.

"The flavor of my Philly sandwich is really good. I haven't tasted the Mayor's turkey dinner, but I think he's done with it. I think the flavor is a little off," Todd said, straight-faced.

"I see," the waitress replied, somewhat unsure of his

answer.

"We're finished here. You can leave the check with the Mayor, he's treating me today," Todd said as he got up from the table.

Fitzgerald forced a smile but said nothing.

~~~

"I heard you had fun in Bozeman," Jerry said to Marky-mark.

"Oh yeah, I'm outta here," Marky said.

"No way. You landed a job while you were out there?" asked Jerry.

"Yup, they have a vacancy and the chief hired me on the spot. He's gotta get official approval from the city council. After that I'll give my two-week notice to Williston and get the hell out of here," Marky replied, with a huge grin on his face.

"Are they hiring any reporters out there?" asked Jerry, half-joking, half not.

"Couldn't tell ya," Marky said, "but like you told me, maybe you should take a vacation and go have a look-see."

"Well, I'm actually thinking of Portland, Oregon. I've been looking on *Craigslist* and there are lots of jobs there. Cost of living is high, but so is the quality of life," Jerry said.

"I've never been there but I hear it's nice. I think you
~~~

should go there. Then I'll have somebody to visit when I'm on vacation," Marky said.

"I'm happy for you man," Jerry extended his hand and they shook.

He's really doing it. Getting the fuck out of Williston.

~~~

Clay Banacek sat in the Raymond James Community Center hot tub. His back was aching from rig-work and the soothing hot water felt good. He watched the kids run around the big pool. They were having fun, jumping, splashing, just being kids. It brought a smile to his face when he thought about them. Their whole lives ahead for them. He reflected on his life and the twists and turns; his bad decisions that had cost him money and years from his lifespan. He knew he had squandered opportunities: jobs, women, businesses. That was the thing about life and self-reflection. It's easy to look back and realize where you messed up; it isn't so easy to see it clearly as you were living it. Do-overs are not allowed.

Learn from your mistakes.

His life-journey was messed up. One thing he *had* managed to learn was how to unwind a position. He liked that term – *unwind your position.* It was a stock-trader phrase, used to describe how they closed out bad trades. It applied to life too.

Clay learned he could unwind positions – his nagging wife, his busted cars, his underwater mortgage – and finally his dead-end job with Milwaukee Engineering.
~~~

Running his life like a stock trader had real upside. He didn't get emotional about things any more. Possessions were unimportant. In fact, he realized possessions only weighed people down, made them heavy in life, with "stuff."

Williston purged him of that. He had nothing with him that wasn't in the trunk of his car. His focus was on the present; the here and now. Not the fantasy-land of the future that may or may not come to fruition. It was good to have goals; strive for something, desire something – otherwise life was meaningless.

Clay's new goal was to find a utilitarian lifestyle without being trapped by possessions. The coveting-madness in the USA was an epidemic. The media fostered it. Billions were spent each year to persuade consumers to *need things.* That they were *less than*, if they didn't *have what their neighbors had.*

Buy more, Build more, Sell more, Be more.

None of it was true. It was a fake reality; a tantalizing Madison-avenue marketing scheme to instill the notion of *I never have enough.* The never-ending parade of titillation for consumers –

Buy this lingerie and you'll have more sex.

Buy this supplement and get ripped muscles.

Buy this workout video and get the body you deserve.

Buy this car so you get noticed.

Clay pulled himself out of the hot-tub and toweled off. As he walked into the men's shower area he noticed it immediately. On the floor, in front of the common shower, was a big Lincoln-Log of human turd.

Clay carefully dodged the turd and walked into the locker room, which was empty – except for a 15-year old boy, who was dressing very slowly, laboriously.

"Hey kid," Clay yelled.

The boy slowly turned his head.

"Did you see that turd in the shower?" Clay asked.

The kid just looked at him with vacant, starring eyes.

"I just want to know, did you see that when you got out of the pool?" Clay asked again as he approached the boy.

The boy didn't respond. The antennae went up in Clay's head.

What the fuck? There's something off with this kid.

Clay went to his locker and quickly changed. He paced himself so he could follow the boy out of the locker room. Ten minutes later the boy lurched to the exit, into the main building. A woman was waiting for him in the lobby. She held his hand and led him slowly towards the front door. Clay stepped up to her.

"Excuse me, is everything okay with the boy?" he asked.

"Well I think so," she said, giving her son a once-over.

"Why do you ask?"

"I tried to talk with him in the locker room and he was distant, non-communicative," Clay replied, not wanting to come off as an asshole or a potential child molester.

"Timmy has autism and he doesn't communicate very well," she said. "He loves coming to the pool after school. Did something happen in the pool?" she asked.

Other than the huge turd in the shower? No, nothing happened.

"Everything's okay. I just wanted to talk to him. You know, just chit-chat," he lied.

"Thank you for trying," she said. "Maybe if he sees you more, he will talk to you. He's very shy," she said as they walked out of the building.

Clay stood there for a moment. It was the right thing to do. *Say nothing.*

~~~

"Did you get the job?" asked Wayne.

"Yup, no piss-test or anything. They hired me on the spot at $28 per hour including medical insurance," Larry said as he combed his hair in the mirror.

"Why are you getting all dressed up?" Wayne asked, "You headed into town?"

"Yup, I got a date." Larry replied.

"A date? How the fuck did you get a date. I haven't
~~~

told you about *my* date yet," Wayne laughed.

"You had a date?" Larry asked.

"Yeah, I met this attorney when I was at the Bakken Gold conference. We had dinner and a few drinks. She's got a possible job opportunity for me. But tell me about your date," Wayne asked.

"Well, when I was in town for the truck driving interview I went into the grocery store to get some Burt's Bee hand lotion. So I'm looking at all the products and this cute gal is shopping the same aisle, we start talking. Anyway, her name is Cindy she owns a dance studio with her sister. So one thing leads to another and we go have a coffee and she gave me her number," Larry explained.

"So she's okay with dating an out-of-state, roustabout-turned-truck driver?" Wayne asked.

"I guess so. Either that or she was likes my good looks," Larry said.

"Well just wait 'til she sees your horse-cock, then she'll *really* be interested," Wayne laughed.

"A man called Horse," Larry laughed.

"Well, good for you. A new job and a new romance," Wayne said.

"Thanks man," Larry said as he turned away from the mirror.

Larry sat on the small chair and looked around the tiny man-camp room that had been their home for the past year. He took out his small brass pipe and packed the bowl with marijuana. Wayne watched him as he lit up and sucked in the marijuana smoke, deep into his lungs, then blew out a steady stream of smoke.

"Getting lit-up before your date?" asked Wayne a bit surprised.

"Yeah why not. When I'm high I'm more relaxed. My brain has better throughput. This oil rig job has dulled my brain. I feel like a mechanical robot. I want to be loose and more alive while I'm out with her. Women pick up on that," Larry explained.

"I'm sure you're right. Whatever works. Maybe she'll smoke with you." Wayne proposed.

"Oh that'd be cool. I'll have to ask her," Larry said.

~~~

Jerry found Lisa stretched out in the backyard watching the birds and critters move around. She had her legs up on the railing and looked incredibly hot, but her face expressed stress.

She was getting ready to pull the plug.

"How's it going?" he asked, knowing full well, it wasn't going well.

"I've had enough of this place. I can't go another month here. It's been a long winter, I've made a good chunk of money, but it's time to go," she said.

"Are you still thinking Portland," Jerry asked.
~~~

"Yeah, there are several art dealers there. I'll connect with one of them," she said.

"Would you like some company on your journey or do you want to go it alone?" he asked.

"What do you mean company? Like ride along with me out there and help me move?" she asked.

"No, I mean roommate-company. Like you and I living together. Going forward in life together," he told her.

"I wasn't sure you'd be interested in hanging with me anymore," she said.

"I'm ready for that if you are," Jerry said. "I like living with you, but I realize I want more than housemate," he laughed, with a dead serious look on his face.

"Yeah? Me too," she said. "I never thought about a relationship with you, but now that we have one, all I think about is how to keep it going," Lisa confided. "That's why I'm still here."

"I feel the same way," Jerry said.

He paused for a moment.

"Seriously, I never thought we'd get involved. This was just a crash-house. But now we are involved. So I guess we either crash-n-burn now or we lock-n-load with each other and see what comes next," he said.

"I want the lock-n-load part," she said, smiling.

She stood up and they hugged for a long passionate kiss.

"Portland, here we come," Lisa said. "Now drop those pants and get in the bedroom."

CHAPTER VI

"Holy fucking shit," Fitzgerald said aloud as he read the newspaper.

Cybak set down his coffee and returned to his vein-clogging bacon-n-eggs breakfast.

"What's the matter?" asked Cybak.

Fitzgerald cautiously looked out from the restaurant booth to make sure no one was listening.

"Fucking OPEC just announced they're going to keep oil production at record levels. I'll read you what it says," Fitzgerald said with a glare in his eyes.

> • West Texas Intermediate fell to a four-year low as Saudi Arabia's oil minister said the price will stabilize by itself. Wall Street analysts were predicting they'd reduce their output in order to keep prices above $80 per barrel.

"What do we care?" asked Cybak nonchalantly.

"Do you trade stocks? Do you have an investment portfolio or do you put your money under the mattress?" Fitzgerald fumed. "I can guarantee you this will affect the here and now of Williston."

"Okay, explain it to me. By the way, I have a Roth 401k retirement, so I'm not a complete idiot when it comes to finance. But I don't trade stocks," Cybak admitted.

"Here's the deal," Fitzgerald said.

"Oil prices have been crashing for the past week. Most people haven't noticed, but I watch that kind of thing. Yesterday, the OPEC ministers met and decided to hold production at current levels...which are high, oil prices fell below $70 a barrel for the first time since 2010."

"See when times are good, we get $100 a barrel for oil. Now $80 oil is bad for the fracking companies, but $70 is a disaster. Not just the Bakken but oil in general," Fitzgerald continued.

"That'll mean cheaper gas prices right?" said Cybak.

"Theoretically, yes," answered Fitzgerald.

"What ya mean by that? Either it is or it isn't," Cybak yelled back. "Whenever the price of oil goes up, the price at the pump goes up immediately. Are you tellin' me that that when oil drops in price, gasoline prices won't follow?"

"Well not right away," said Fitzgerald. "See these oil companies; they always hedge their investments by selling forward, to guarantee a certain price per barrel. So, let's say EOG wanted to insure they could get $90 a barrel; they could open a contract to deliver and be guaranteed that price for their oil. That way, if oil falls to $80 a barrel they still get paid $90. If oil goes to $110, they still get $90."

"So it's like a double-edge sword?" Cybak stated.

"No, it's not. That's a horrible analogy," replied Fitzgerald.

"So, what is a good analogy then?" asked Cybak, now pissed off.

"I don't have a good analogy, but I can offer up an axiom," Fitzgerald replied.

"REDUCE THE CHANCES OF A NEGATIVE OUTCOME."

"What you'd call CYA – Cover Your Ass!" Fitzgerald laughed.

"They need to insure they make a profit, so they lock it in at a certain price; otherwise the oil analysts would criticize them for being imprudent and not cautious enough with bond holder's investments, maybe the stockholders too, at some point," Fitzgerald continued.

"So what does this have to do with the Bakken?" asked Cybak.

"Fracking becomes a losing venture below $65 a barrel. That's a big deal. We are looking at the headlights of a crash like we had in 1986. Don't you remember when things went to shit then?" continued Fitzgerald.

"These fracking companies out here; I'm not talking Exxon or BP, I'm talking Continental, EOG, Kodiak, Hess. They finance their operations by selling junk bonds. LOTS of junk bonds."

"Yeah, what about it?" asked Cybak, clearly not comprehending any of it.

"If these fracking operations lose money, they won't be able to pay the interest payments on the junk bonds – which will put them in default, which will lead directly to bankruptcy. When that happens, or actually long *before* the bankruptcies occur, this oil-play in North Dakota will be over," Fitzgerald concluded.

"What's next?" ask Cybak.

"What's next for me is a meeting with a man-camp lobbyist from East Coast Logistics," Fitzgerald said.

"What's that all about?" replied Cybak.

"They want to bypass the county's moratorium on man-camps, so he's coming to my office to see if I can help in the process or if the city of Williston can annex more land adjacent to town for a build site," Fitzgerald said.

"You keep me in the loop on that," Cybak said.

"Yeah right, just like you kept me in the loop on the Colorado developer," Fitzgerald shot back.

"I thought that was water under the bridge? We're both going to get paid. Stop worrying," Cybak retorted.

"When you bring me the suitcase of money I'll relax," Fitzgerald said.

The waitress swung by their table to top off their coffees.

"How's everything tasting?" she asked.

"We tasted everything," Fitzgerald barked.

The waitress glared at him.

"What you should be asking is 'how is the flavor?' That's what you want to know. Why does every damn waitress in the country ask 'how's everything tasting?'

Who started that? Did you get that from a sit-com?" Fitzgerald barked.

The waitress turned away seething mad.

The Mayor is such a dick.

~~~

Fitzgerald sat in office waiting for the lobbyist. He was agitated and wanted to soothe his nerves with some porn on his computer. He couldn't use the city computer because the Nazi-like IT administrator tracked internet activity. After reading a few articles on *Zerohedge*, he pulled out his Android to watch porn. It would eat up his monthly data usage but he didn't care. He spun through some pictures and found a few enjoyable ones.

Some amazing tattoo work on these young women.

His fun was interrupted when the secretary came to his door. She had a scowl on her face.

"Your one o'clock appointment is here," she said as she walked out.

Fitzgerald didn't bother standing up from his desk; whoever the guy was, he could just find his way in and take a chair. He couldn't have been more wrong.

The first thing he noticed was the sound of her high-heeled shoes approaching his office. She was tall, blond like Monroe, maybe forty, with a skimpy, tight-fitting skirt, long legs, and red come-fuck-me shoes.

Jesus fucking Christ, this woman is gorgeous.
~~~

"Mayor Fitzgerald," she said as she approached his desk, "I'm Maggie Bleven."

He stood up and gently shook her hand. He didn't want to crush it, didn't want to wimp it; he needed to exert just the right pressure and duration to show her he was interested in her sexually. He took her hand; it was soft with good grip. He hung on a second or two longer than normal; like the gay handshake without the palm rub. If she got the message, she didn't show it.

"Are you related to Bert?" he quipped.

"No, but people ask me that all the time," she laughed. "He was a baseball player or something like that."

Fitzgerald glanced at his phone to make sure the porn was off his screen.

"Yes, Bert Bleven was a pitcher for Minnesota Twins. He had the nastiest curveball in the Major Leagues," Fitzgerald recited. "I saw him throw a curve ball to a Cleveland Indian hitter by the name of Oscar Grumble. Oscar thought the pitch was going to hit him in the ribs, so he jumps out of the batter's box, only to have the umpire call it a strike."

"I'm from East Coast Logistics," she said, ignoring the lame baseball reminisce. "I've been hired to work out arrangements for the construction of a new man camp. Preferably next to the city of Williston," she said.

"As you know, there is a moratorium on man camps both in the city and county. We would have to work out something special if annexation was going to occur," Fitzgerald said.

"That's why I'm here. To work out something *special*," she smiled at him.

Is she going to fuck me to get this deal done?

"East Coast believes the moratorium should be eased a bit, to meet the needs of the mining operators in this region. As you know these man-camps are portable operations. They're like a Band-Aid to help accommodate the heavy manpower needs in a temporary way," she said.

"We are running out of water, sewer, electricity," Fitzgerald countered. "It's not just a matter of the city council giving a thumbs-up. We have limits to what our existing infrastructure can provide and support. We have roughly 10,000 man-camp beds in the county now. You're proposal is seeking an additional 4,000 beds. That's forty-percent increase."

"There are solutions to every problem, Mr. Fitzgerald. Sometimes the easiest way to solve vexing issues is to throw money at the problem," Maggie countered.

As much as he wanted to fuck-the-hell out of her, he knew she was asking too much. There was no way to push through a 4,000-bed build-out with the city's current facilities.

"Are you familiar with Dickenson? Do you know what happened out there?" Fitzgerald asked.

"No, I'm not aware of their situation," she said.

"Let me tell you what happened in Dickenson. I know the story well because I was living out there at the time," Fitzgerald said.

"Twenty years ago North Dakota had its first oil boom. Were you aware of that?" he asked.

"I thought this was the oil-boom?" Maggie said with puzzlement.

"Oh no, this is the second boom. See, in the first boom, Dickenson, which is in the very southwest region of the oil patch, overbuilt to accommodate the oil industry. The boom was chugging along and everyone was excited and making money and Dickenson built out their paved roads, sewer system, water supplies, sidewalks; things like that," Fitzgerald lectured.

"Then, almost overnight the price of oil collapsed and the boom ended. The music stopped and City of Dickenson had no chair. Dickenson was left holding the bag on $19 million dollars of overbuilt infrastructure payments. The oil companies left town, the transient boomers left the state, and the taxes on homeowners and businesses skyrocketed. They had to pay off the bills for outsiders who had left town. They had roads and sidewalks to nowhere," he stated.

Maggie listened intently, nodding her head.

"We don't want that to happen here, in Williston. If you haven't noticed, the price of oil is sagging as of late," Fitzgerald mentioned.

"Mr. Fitzgerald, I'm certain this boom is here to stay. The geologists confirm there are billions of barrels of oil here. The oil companies are all represented here. This time it will last. Oil prices are high and will stay high. Oil consumption is also high. Any dip is just a temporary fluctuation. Once they get the pipeline built, oil will flow from this region for the next twenty years," she recited from a memorized corporate briefing.

"Ms. Bleven, I agree with what you are saying, but my job as the Mayor is to look out for the best interests of the people of Williston. What are you prepared to bring to the table?"

"East Coast Logistics has very deep pockets. We work hand-in-hand with many of the major oil companies. I'm sure we can work out a mutual arrangement on this," she said.

"Are you available for dinner tonight?" she asked. "I arrived by commuter jet and I'm staying at the Grand. Perhaps you know of a nice restaurant where I can take you for dinner and drinks and we can get down to brass tacks. I'm leaving tomorrow afternoon so I don't have a lot of time," she said.

"Sure, I would love to have dinner with you. I'll make reservations and pick you up at say five o'clock," Fitzgerald said.

"Splendid. I'll see you then," she said, getting up from the desk.

He watched her walk out of his office and out into the street. She was put together like the finest showgirl in Vegas. This was going to be a wonderful evening. He was going to enjoy touching her as much as fondling his gold bars.

~~~

Fitzgerald took his Lexus to the edge of city limits.
~~~

The Williams County plat book opened on the front seat. He studied the various parcels and tried to formulate a plan. Typical annexations were a minimum of 240 acres, so he focused on areas of that size.

After an hour of exploring possible man-camp locations, he found the perfect layout. Sitting on the southwest edge of town was a four-hundred acre field. The tract was accessible by road and had electrical power and sewer. There was one complication; the hundred-year-old First Lutheran Church was sitting on the property. He drove past the church and looked at it from different angles. It was smack-dab in the middle of the section he needed.

This will do nicely. The church will have to catch fire in the middle of the night.

Three hours later he picked up Ms. Bleven from the Grand Williston hotel. They had dinner at the The Williston restaurant. The eatery was supposedly the "best in town" for fine dining, but Fitzgerald knew the food was second-rate and over-priced, but restaurant choices were limited; they weren't in Chicago.

He had a plan, but decided to play it cool with the knock-out lobbyist. They sent her around the country to close deals. She was highly compensated, addicted to money and nice things; she would do whatever was necessary to get this mission accomplished. He laughed to himself as he thought about squeezing Todd the "tattoo artist" for money. Maggie was low-hanging fruit; he was going to *taste* the fruit flavor.

The next morning he rolled out of her king-sized bed

and landed on weak legs. She was, as he predicted, a tiger in the sack. She fucked him for over an hour after dinner and again at five a.m. He couldn't take any more. She was sound asleep as he dressed and headed out the door. He slipped out the side door and into his Lexus.

Maggie was a great ride, a "good strap" as his college buddies used to say. She wasn't bedding him for fun or love – it was all about the money. She wanted one thing – approval for a four-thousand bed man camp. He loved capitalism, the give and take, the *quid quo pro.* He couldn't imagine another way of life. Everything cost something; everyone had a price; he liked it that way.

~~~

Fitzgerald banged the gavel to call the meeting of the Williston City Council to order. The first speaker was Lew Dodge, the city Administrator.

"I'm here to give report and call the council's attention to a few issues. First is the issue of nuisance 911 calls. Our latest report shows that we had more than twelve-thousand emergency calls, half those originated within the city limits. The problem is the nuisance calls are increasing. This wastes the dispatcher's time and clogs the telephone lines – which could hamper a response to a real emergency. We've had one individual call twenty-five separate times for non-emergencies. This is not what 911 is for."

"I understand your concern, but let me ask you this," Fitzgerald said. "It's my understanding that nuisance calls, false calls, etcetera are misdemeanors."
~~~

"That's correct," replied Dodge.

"So what are the police doing about these nuisance calls?" Fitzgerald asked.

"We haven't asked the police for help. They're busy with other matters," Dodge replied.

"Well if you don't want to have the police issue citations and stop the problem, why are you wasting the time of the city council?" Fitzgerald retorted.

"I ah, thought it was the right thing to do. To inform the council of the situation," Dodge said.

"Do you have anything else to report?" asked the Mayor.

"Yes, the next item to report is that the city has collected approximately $350,000 in fines for the year, which is an increase year over year of $100,000 dollars," Dodge stated proudly.

"Thank you Mr. Dodge for your report," Fitzgerald said, happy to dismiss the underling.

"Our next item is a request to speak from bar owner Dennis Buchholz about a food trailer request," Fitzgerald stated.

A gruff, salty-dog in a plaid shirt walked to the podium to address the Council.

"My name is Dennis Buchholz, I own the Old Saloon in town. Most of you know me," he chuckled.

"I'm here to make *another* request to operate my food

trailer in town. As you know the restaurants in Williston are overwhelmed with long lines and slow service. I have converted a mobile home into a food wagon, complete with stove, water system and waste storage. I've had it inspected and it is ready to operate. My goal is to provide the city with quality food service and create jobs. This is the second time I have requested a special use permit to operate in the city of Williston," he finished.

Fitzgerald and Cybak were stoned-faced; Buchholz had been given every opportunity to make a deal with either of them but he refused to play ball. So now they were sitting on his request, doing nothing with it until he *greased the wheel* with some back-channel cash.

"Are there any questions or concerns I can answer today, to help move this forward. Time's a wasting. I want to get this permit approved and begin serving food in Williston," Buchholz stated, now a bit irritated.

"Thank you for bringing this to our attention," Cybak said. "We will need more time to weigh the pros and cons of your request."

"You gotta be kidding me," Buchholz said in a louder voice. "I've waited three months already. That's plenty of time to get this matter resolved."

Fitzgerald decided to shut him down.

"Thank you for bringing this issue to the front burner," Fitzgerald stated calmly, as he moved some papers around.

"Our next item is discussion of the eviction notices to the thirty residents of Parkway Apartments," Fitzgerald read.

Buchholz realized his time was finished. He looked confused, glared at Cybak and walked out of the room.

A group of five people came up the microphone and prepared to make statements.

"My name is Rhonda Smith, I've lived in Parkway Apartments for eight years. I have four children and I've just been evicted, as were the other twenty-nine residents of Parkway. We were given notices last month to move out by the first. This eviction is unreasonable and un-American, and we ask the city council to stop the eviction process," she stated.

"Mrs. Smith," Fitzgerald said, "we have empathy for your situation, but Parkway is not owned by the city. It's owned by a private party or a corporation. I don't know the details but you could look up the owners at the Williams County Treasurer office. I'm sure the owners have a valid reason to remove the tenants."

"So you won't help us? You're the Mayor, can't you do something?" she asked.

"Being Mayor is not the same thing as an Emperor or a King," Fitzgerald laughed, "There are times I wish I was the King of Williston."

The council and some audience members laughed, but Smith did not. She looked that the others and they stormed out of the room.

"We're not making our constituents very happy tonight," Fitzgerald said. "Hopefully we can turn that around."

"Our next item is an up-down vote on the proposal to construct a man-camp on the Boone property on the edge of town. This was a pre-moratorium proposal which means it is grandfathered-in and is exempt from the moratorium," Fitzgerald lied.

There was no discussion on the vote and it passed unanimously. Even Gaylor voted for it.

"Our last order of business tonight is a proposal by Chief of police, "Tiger" Johnson to acquire surplus military equipment for the police department," Fitzgerald said.

A burly cop in his 50's with a belly that flopped over his belt ambled up to the podium with some papers.

"We have the opportunity to acquire surplus military equipment at no cost to the city. This equipment is available through the Department of Defense, authorized by Congress to transfer military hardware to civilian police departments to fight the "war on drugs" and the "war on terror," Johnson recited.

"Our proposal, requests a Mine Resistant Ambush Protected vehicle, armored vests, night vision equipment, M-16 rifles, ammunition, and several silencers. We are preparing for something that may never happen, and we can take advantage of these federal programs at no charge to the tax-payers," Johnson said.

Councilman Gaylor cleared his throat before speaking.

"Why do we need this combat equipment? Do we really want small town cops dressing in black ninja SWAT clothing? Parading around with automatic weapons on a military truck? Police departments are tasked with keeping the peace, not presenting a paramilitary show of force."

Chief Johnson was taken aback; he expected the request to slide through with no opposition.

"We have military veterans coming home from Iraq and Afghanistan who know how to build improvised explosive devices. This equipment would protect our officers. This is all about safety," Johnson countered.

"I don't think this is about safety," Gaylor said. "I think this is about the military-industrial complex finding a way to sell more military product to the government. I think they want to sell new equipment so they need to get rid of the old equipment. Instead of scrapping it, they offer it to law enforcement agencies throughout the country."

Gaylor paused for effect.

"Chief, let me ask you. Have you had a problem with military veterans making homemade I.E.D's ? Have you heard of any veterans making I.E.D's and planting them in small towns? What I read about, is veterans killing themselves from post-traumatic stress. I've never read anything about veterans becoming terrorists," Gaylor barked.

The Chief was speechless.

"Frankly, I think your logic is stupid. And I'm offended that you would utter a statement in public that our veterans are potential terrorists. They did the same thing when the Vietnam vets returned. The television shows were full of plots about the crazy Vietnam veteran who shoots up a town. Nothing could be further from the truth," Gaylor continued.

"We execute search warrants from time to time and this equipment would be useful for that," said Chief Johnson. "Last year I went to Los Angeles for the Urban Shield trade show. There are police forces around the country, getting grants for this type of weaponry. Many of the police departments are using asset forfeiture money to purchase equipment," Johnson stated.

"Just because you can, doesn't mean you should," added Gaylor. "And I don't believe asset forfeiture is Constitutional."

"I'm just trying to save the taxpayers the cost of getting state-of-the-art equipment," Johnson retorted.

"I think we've all seen the images on television of militarized police departments smashing down doors, fighting people in the streets, conducting these military raids on civilians. I am opposed to this and I see no need for Williston's peace officers to indulge themselves in this type of pseudo-military equipment," Gaylor said.

The Chief stood there speechless. His face was red; he knew he wasn't going to get the new toys for the department. One thing was certain, he was gonna stick it to Gaylor.

Fucking atheist is gonna slip in the shower.

"Thank you for your presentation, Chief Johnson," Fitzgerald said. "We will now adjourn this meeting."

Fitzgerald grabbed Cybak's arm as he was leaving the meeting.

"When can I expect my suitcase for the Boone-camp?" Fitzgerald said firmly.

"They gave me half down. I'll get the rest within the week. Believe me, they're gung-ho to get this going – you'll get your money," Cybak said.

"Hey listen, I'm working on another deal. I'm going to need your help on it. It's only in the preliminary stage, but I think it's going to be a good one," Fitzgerald said with excitement.

Cybak's eyes opened wide. "Another one? So soon?" he asked.

"It is what it is. Make hay while the sun is shining. Remember what I said about oil dropping. We need to make hay right now, the sun is still out," Fitzgerald said.

"You can count on me," Cybak said, smiling as he walked away.

CHAPTER VII

"Fuck you, you fucking fuck," yelled Gaylor at Police Chief Johnson.

Johnson tapped Gaylor on the chest for the second time, and yelled back, "Listen you atheist fuck. You ever talk to me like that again I'm gonna take you outside and dust you off."

"Don't just telegraph it asshole, bring it." Gaylor shot back. "Do you want me to put my hands up so you can shoot me?"

Chief Johnson started at Gaylor.

This fucker has a lot of balls to talk to me like that.

"You're one of those guys, eh?" the Chief said back. "You want me to slap you down so you can sue me and collect six figures from an insurance settlement."

"No, what I really want is for you to hit me – so I can retaliate and beat your bully-ass into the ground – in front of people," Gaylor said.

"Oh you're gonna kick my ass are ya," Chief Johnson retorted.

Johnson noticed the *dead serious* look in Gaylor's eye. He also noticed, for the first time, that Gaylor had a set of pipes on him.

Was this fucker tattooed? Was he a trained fighter? A UFC-type guy who could ground-pound a guys' face with his elbows?

The Chief tried to relax, he needed to deescalate this. He hadn't been in a fight in four years and was in no kind of shape the fight a guy who worked-out regularly.

"All I'm saying is this – that was an embarrassing incident," Chief Johnson replied. "In the future I would ask that you not berate me in front of other people."

"I understand what you're saying," replied Gaylor, "but I don't believe you are sincere."

"Why's that?" countered the Chief.

"I've seen your type of personality before. You use the power of your badge and your authority to intimidate people. You are really a very insecure man. That's why you became a cop in the first place. Now that you're the Chief, you feel you have even more power over people. You probably push people around all the time and nobody ever pushes back. Am I right?" asked Gaylor.

"What is your problem with me Mr. Gaylor?" the Chief asked.

"I don't have a problem with you personally. It's just the personality type you represent. There are millions of men and probably women, just like you. They're always pushing the little people around. The moment they get an ounce of authority, they wield it like switch, whipping people on their bottoms whenever they get the chance," Gaylor shot back.

"Let me ask you this Chief; why do insult me about my atheism? I don't call you a "Lutheran fuck," or a "Jewish fuck," Gaylor yelled out.

"Well, I simply don't like atheists. The Lord Jesus is the Way and I believe that," the Chief responed calmly.

"You can believe in any cock-and-bull mythology you want," replied Gaylor, "but you show yourself as a real bigot when you criticize other belief systems. I thought you were a good American?"

"I am a good American and this is and always has been a Christian county," the Chief said proudly.

"Yeah right. Nothing could be further from the truth," said Gaylor. "The Constitution is a secular document. There's no mention of Christianity or Jesus Christ."

"Is that so?" asked the Chief. "Are you telling me the Founding Fathers were non-believers?"

"Some of the Founding Fathers were believers. They were not against religion. They were against Church-State partnerships because they knew what trouble occurred in Europe from alliances between religion and government," Gaylor stated.

"I'm not going to stand here and debate religion with you Mr. Gaylor," the Chief said.

"Fine with me, Chief," Gaylor said. "Just so we're clear; if you insult my faith again – which is atheism, I'm going to drop you to the mat and open up some cuts on your face."

"You're quite an asshole, Mr. Gaylor. I will be sure to avoid you like the plague in the future. This is the last conversation we are ever gonna have," replied the Chief.

"I expected you'd say that. That's what bullies do. They back away from real confrontations. They're scared to fight when it comes down to it," Gaylor yelled back at him.

The Chief shook his head – the same way his parents did when they wanted to show how disappointing he was to them. He turned and walked away.

~~~

"Your shelves are getting low," said Leroy Lind.

"I've been so busy with things that I haven't had the time to re-order inventory," Fitzgerald lied. He had no intentions of keeping the shelves full. As items sold off; all the better. He was leaving town soon.

"Heard your house is up for sale," Lind asked.

"Already sold. The closing is today," Fitzgerald said.

"Did you get what you wanted for it?" asked Lind.

"Yeah, I got $190,000 for it," Fitzgerald said, knowing he might as well admit the amount, the transaction would be in the newspaper anyway.

"What are you going to do now? You going to build something in the country?" asked Lind.

"Maybe. I'm considering all my options at this point," Fitzgerald answered.

Fitzgerald looked at his watch; he was tired of the prying conversation.
~~~

"I gotta go get some paperwork before the closing, I'll see you tomorrow," Fitzgerald said as he headed toward the door.

He really did have some paperwork to pick up before the closing. He couldn't wait to get his hands on the check. His house had only cost $52,000 when he bought it. He was going to pocket a nice chunk today; probably $100,000 after all the closing costs, commissions and fees were pulled out.

More gold bars! More Vegas money!

He got in the Lexus and drove to the edge of town to have another look at the First Lutheran Church. As he pulled up next to the church he noticed two cars parked in the back.

Probably a couple ladies cleaning up after the Sunday service.

He parked out front and walked up the wide front steps to the door. He was hoping it wasn't locked. He wanted a last look at the alter and pulpit – *before he burned it down.*

The 12-foot door opened easily and he stepped inside the dark church. He heard a noise from inside somewhere, kind of a "yelp."

That sounded weird.

Fitzgerald walked to the side aisle, up the outer wall alongside the pews. The thick carpet made his steps inaudible.

"Ahh," the voice rang out from the front of the church.

He heard panting and connected the dots.

People were fucking on the altar of the church.

He stopped in his tracks. He didn't want to get busted, but whoever was up there, didn't want to get busted either. If he recognized whoever was up there fucking, he could *leverage* them.

Fitzgerald tiptoed to the front and peered over the railing. On the bright red carpet, the young church secretary was on her hands-n-knees while Pastor Braun put the wood to her from behind.

Thrill-seeking Jesus people.

He watched for a few moments before backing out of the church and returning to his car. He drove off feeling sexually charged, wondering how he could take advantage this new information.

Pastor didn't have a pot to piss in.

Secretary was a married, ugly-mutt.

He couldn't see any angle. He opened his laptop, connected to the internet, and Googled "pastor Leo Braun." Amazingly, Braun's name came up on *BlackCollarCrimes.* This was not the first time Braun had swung his dick with a parishoner. He had been ousted twice – both times for having sexual contact with members of his church. It was clear, the elders of First Lutheran had not done any due-diligence before hiring their dick-swinging pastor.

Fitzgerald contemplated.

Could he extort a couple thousand bucks from Braun? Maybe, but life was too complicated at the moment.

~~~

"Hey Big Country," Jerry yelled at Marky-Mark as he drove by in his squad car.

Mark pulled the squad car over to the side of the road as Jerry stepped off the sidewalk to talk.

"When are you leaving?" Jerry asked.

"This Saturday," Mark replied.

"Do you need any help?" asked Jerry.

"Nope, just my household stuff. No furniture. I'll buy what I need in Bozeman," Mark replied.

"It has been fun," Jerry said, shaking hands with Mark, "I'd say I'm going to miss you but I'm leaving too."

"You're going to Portland then? You and the stripper staying together?" Marky asked with a hound-dog grin.

"Yup, we're heading out at the end of July. I gave my notice to the newspaper. You know, I've been here nearly a year, and I've never met Ditzy," Jerry said.

"Well I guess she's riding horses all the time," Mark said.

"Well, I hope we can party together sometime. Either in Portland or Bozeman," Mark said.
~~~

"Or both," Jerry responded. "I have your e-mail address, we'll keep in touch. See you 'round."

Marky-Mark drove the squad back into the street and headed down the block.

Jerry mulled it over as he kept walking towards the *Daily* office. Williston wasn't a community any more. It was a populace. The locals had been driven out; replaced by workers and businesses that were only there to make money – not to form a community.

Had it always been like that?

Did boom towns replace real towns – then fade out and return to a real town again.

He thought about his future. He had never lived with a woman before. Life with Lisa as roommate had been so easy. What would a real relationship be like? They had *stumbled* into their relationship, but now they were *choosing* to continue it.

How was that going to work?

Does anyone know how their relationship will work? Will it stick? Will it crash-n-burn?

He thought about his Uncle Bill – liquored up and running his mouth in the fishing boat:

Life is short Jerry. You have to go for it.

He strode into the *Daily* office realizing he *had* accomplished something. He had been *part* of something – a boomtown. Coming out to Williston was a challenge; leaving Williston was a no-brainer. There was nothing here. It would remain a boomtown for as long as the oil extraction took place. Then it would fold up like a cheap tent; the remnants wouldn't be pretty.

Detroit on the prairie.

It was time to write an editorial about his experience. Gloria was gone and the office was quiet. He turned on his computer and began typing.

WELCOME TO THE BOOMTOWN

by Jerry Ebson

~~~

"You're getting engaged? You're shitting me?" Wayne exclaimed.

"For real," Larry said.

"Cindy pregnant or what?" asked Wayne.

"No she's not pregnant. We just want to go to the next level," Larry said defensively.

"Careful Major," Wayne said, using his favorite line from *Where Eagles Dare.*

"She owns a house in town. She's a trust-fund kid ya know. Money is no issue with her," Larry said.

Wayne nodded his head.

"So, yeah…I'm moving in with her and we're going to start a life together. I'll keep driving water truck and she's got the dance studio. It's all gonna work out. Maybe do
~~~

that for a while, make bank, get married, then move to Hawaii," Larry said.

"That sounds great. I'm happy for you," Wayne said, a bit perplexed by Larry's sudden homie attitude.

He's only been divorced a year. Why rush into another marriage?

"What are you going to do?" asked Larry. "Are you still in contact with that fracking attorney?"

"Yes, I sent my resume to her same company. They need organizers and advocates based in their Seattle office. I've had enough of Williston. I've saved about forty-grand, I can coast on that for a while. I know Seattle is expensive-as-fuck, but it's a cool place to live," Wayne said.

"When are you leaving?" asked Larry.

"As soon as we complete this last well. I told the rig manager I'd be leaving after that," Wayne said.

"Is that Gene? Is he still the rig manager," asked Larry.

"Fuck no, Gene was fired for that illegal dumping of hot-sand at that rancher's place. I guess the EPA got wind of that, some tipster called, and they busted that rancher and he spilled the beans. Gene was fired and the company got fined a couple-hundred thousand," Wayne related.

"Serves 'em right. Those guys dumping that shit out there like that," Larry laughed.

"Just glad that you and I didn't get pulled into that; Gene's the only person that went down," Wayne said.

"You have my phone number and email. So if you and your fiancée want to see Seattle sometime, be sure to look me up," Wayne said holding out his hand for a shake.

"Will do buddy," Larry replied. "It's been fun. Exceeded expectations."

~~~

"You got my fucking money?" Fitzgerald asked Cybak.

"It's right here," Cybak said as he soft-tossed a plastic garbage bag to Fitzgerald.

Cybak had pulled his truck alongside Fitzgerald's Lexus. They selected a rendezvous site outside of Williston; a gravel road in the country, far out of town so they wouldn't be seen.

Fitzgerald frowned at the delivery package; he was used to fake-leather suitcases. Cybak had no class; he was nothing more than a prairie philistine.

"Tell me about your next deal. The man-camp you need my help with," asked Cybak.

"That deal is off the table. I've been trying to reach my contact but my calls and emails haven't been returned.

Maggie had sent a terse email stating East Coast Logistics was no longer interested in building a man-camp.

"Are they spooked on account of oil dropping?" Cybak asked.

"That's my guess. This downturn in price of West
~~~

Texas Crude doesn't look short-term. I think we may be in for a big set-back. Maybe an implosion," Fitzgerald said calmly.

"That bad huh," Cybak muttered.

"It is very bad. The bond yields have doubled, the price of oil is under $60 and still falling. The entire Bakken range is in danger. So is Eagle Ford and every other damn fracking site. If this continues, things are going to collapse around here and I don't want to be around when that happens," Fitzgerald explained.

"How would you like to be the Mayor of Williston?" asked Fitzgerald.

"Bullshit, you're going to quit?" asked Cybak.

"Yeah, I've been thinking this is as good a time as any for me to get out of Dodge. We've had a good run of it. We can all leave town a lot richer than when we came into it," Fitzgerald explained.

"Look, once the contraction begins, it's going to get really ugly around here. The citizens have left; forced out by the high cost of living. Can you image all these empty man camps sitting around? Or the twenty soon-to-be empty hotels? The drilling is going to stop. The trucks, the trains…they're going to disappear. They cannot make money on the Bakken oil below $60. When it goes below $50, the oil companies and service companies are going to pull out. The wells that are producing now will continue until they're depleted. After that, no new wells," said Fitzgerald.

"I just can't believe this is happening," Cybak said with

alarm. "We had such a sweet thing going here."

"Yeah, those fucking Saudis are smart. They have a plan to cripple the fracking industry. It's working. This play is going to shut down and the boom will be over," Fitzgerald said.

"Who's going to get stuck holding the bag for all the infrastructure costs in Williston?" asked Cybak.

"Well it ain't going to be me. I just sold my house. I'm liquid and my boogie-bag is packed. You might want to think about things differently; get a new perspective," Fitzgerald suggested.

"I think you're right. And to answer your question – *fuck no*, I don't want your Mayor job. If you're getting out, then I want out too," Cybak stated.

"See you later," Fitzgerald said as he got back in his Lexus with the garbage bag of cash.

~~~

Jerry put the last bag of clothing into the trunk of Lisa's Jetta. They didn't have much; just their clothes, their laptops, and some cooking pots and pans. Everything else they would buy in Portland. They cleaned up the kitchen, hauled the trash to the curb and took one final look at the house.

"I'm glad we're getting the hell out of here," Lisa said.

"Me too," Jerry said. "Williston is played-out for us. On to whatever is next," he said as he slipped into the driver's side and started the car.
~~~

"Do you need to stop at the post office to get money orders?" Jerry asked.

"Yes, I have $5,000 cash in the gym bag. I've converted the other fifty-k to money orders already," Lisa said.

"That's a smart way to do it. No IRS records, no taxable income. You stripper girls are smarter than the average bear, I'll say that," Jerry said, laughing.

"It's a way of life for us. We're not going to give Uncle Sam or the state a cut of our money. No way," she replied.

"So here's the deal. I will buy three, $1,000 money orders. You buy the other two. I can't get more than three in one day or it triggers some kind of alert with the government," Lisa explained.

"The government imposes money-order limits as a way of fighting terrorists and drug dealers? Like these lower limits are going to stop anyone. Too funny," Jerry laughed.

After thirty minutes in the post office, they left with a mitt-full of thousand-dollar money orders.

"Okay, do we have everything?" Lisa asked.

"We have food, a cooler full of beer, two bottles of vodka, and Highway 2 is straight ahead. We're golden," Jerry said.

"Goodbye fucking Williston," Lisa yelled out the window.

~~~

Fitzgerald walked into his Mayor's office for the last time. He boxed up a few pictures and mementos and drafted his Letter of Resignation. After printing it out and proofing it, he opened the lid on his PC. The hard-drive needed formatting but he didn't have time to fuck with it. He decided it was easier to remove it and take it out the door. By the time the IT-guy got around to dealing with his PC, he'd be long gone. Fitzgerald pulled the cover, disconnected the wires and popped out the hard drive.

Throw this fucker in the Missouri River.

With the box of memorabilia tucked under his arm, he walked out of the office and didn't look back. Nostalgia was not in his blood. As he passed the secretary's desk he dropped the envelope with his resignation letter in her inbox. He had timed his departure for lunch-time, so she wouldn't be around. He never liked her anyway. She was always such a bitch.

As he neared the front door, he decided to do something symbolic; he needed to. He went over to the light switches and turned them all off. There were other people in the main floor working but he didn't give a shit. Somebody would put them back on again.

He pushed open the glass door and walked to the Lexus. It was fully loaded with his belongings– including his suitcases full of cash and gold bars. Highway 85 would take him south, to Rapid City, and then Denver. In Denver he would buy a pound of marijuana, then drive west into Utah and descend into Nevada. He had already
~~~

rented a luxury condo in the Summerlin area of Las Vegas.

The Lexus moved slowly out of town. As he neared the final stop light before the road opened up, he rolled down his window and yelled at some bystanders.

"THIS CITY IS FUCKED."

EPILOGUE

The Amtrak train clicked along with peaceful repetition. Wayne looked out the window at the vacant North Dakota prairie. It was all the same, everything east of Ike Walton's lodge, just outside of Glacier – was flat, boring prairie. There were herds of buffalo once, and before that – dinosaurs. The fossils recorded life on the prairie for millions of years, long before humans got there. However they got there.

What was once old is new again.

He glanced around at the other people in the passenger car and wondered about their lives, their destinations, and their fate.

Were they coming or going?

He opened the newspaper someone had left in the dining car. The headline grabbed his attention.

Crisis in the Bakken – Oil Falls to 7-Year Low

> Prices at the pump fell across the nation, as the world wide glut of oil continues to push the price of oil lower. The Bakken "oil patch" supplies a million barrels of oil per day. Oil that once sold for $100 a barrel is now in the $40's.
>
> Oil companies continue to scale back operations. Pink slips have gone out en masse as oil companies cancel drilling operations and expansion comes to a halt. Continental, the

largest lease holder, has experienced a brutal stock price decline—as have Whiting, Hess, Oasis and other regional operators.

Frack Sand Suppliers Smashed !

Wisconsin-based Silica Sands Energy has seen it shares tumble from a high of $145, to less than $10 per share. The company, which had a $17 IPO a year earlier, was a favorite of speculators and flavor-of-the-month hedge funds.

Many investors were puzzled by the stock run-up equivalent to a $3.5 billion valuation, for a company that has $50 million negative cash flow. The Wisconsin gravel pits that Wall Street valued like gold mines were in reality, only sand pits.

Three hours later the train stopped in Williston. The red-stone depot was familiar and the Great Northern steam engine was still on display. Wayne looked around for Larry. He pulled out Larry's wedding invitation from his sport coat. The ceremony was Saturday at 11:30 am in the First Lutheran Church.

"Hey Asshole," Larry yelled from the parking lot.

Wayne grabbed his luggage and walked to Larry's car. They shook hands and had a brief hug.

"How are you man?" Wayne asked. "Congratulations on the wedding."

"You're here for a reason, remember that," Larry said. "I need a best-man and you're it."

"I'm here and ready to perform my duty," Wayne replied.

"Thanks for coming. If it wasn't for you; dragging me out to Williston in the first place, I wouldn't be getting married again," Larry said.

"I'm not sure if you're blaming me or giving me credit," Wayne laughed.

"Both, you bastard," laughed Larry.

"It's all good. Cindy and I have a great time together. She's super-easy to be around," Larry bragged.

"Are you still dating the lawyer-lady in Seattle?" Larry asked.

"Not anymore. That kind of fizzled out. It's all good, we're still friends. I'm not very good with female emotions and drama. Just not healed enough from my last situation to deal with that again," Wayne replied.

"I get it," Larry said. "Let's drive around town. I want to show you what's happened here. You won't believe it."

They got into a Ford minivan and drove around town.

"The first thing you might notice," Larry said, "there ain't no traffic."

Wayne nodded his head.

"All the water trucks are gone; the trains with sand have vanished. The town has come to a complete standstill. Look at all the "for sale" signs and vacancies. See that strip mall there? They just built that last year. Now the tenants are gone. No more Japanese steakhouse, no more Western-wear clothing. This place has imploded," Larry explained.

"What about life for you and Cindy?" Wayne asked.

"Lost my water truck job six months ago. Everyone got pink slips and the owner went bankrupt. He had leveraged himself to the max with credit, to buy as many trucks, and hire as many drivers as possible. Like pressing your bet on a craps table. When the seven comes up, you lose everything. That's what's happened to all the businesses here. They were all *pressing their bets;* gambling that it would keep going and going. Nobody saw this oil glut situation happening," Larry explained.

"Look at this school," Larry said. "Cost $50 million to build. We were overrun with school children; now there are no kids around to go to the new school," Larry explained.

They drove on and stopped by the community center.

"Here's the community center," Larry stated, "They added on. Huge expansion with a lazy river and a 135-foot water slide. Spent big bucks on it but they had to close it down because nobody has money to spend."

"What about the man-camps? What did Continental do with our trailer?" Wayne asked.

"Gone. They're all gone. The logistics companies that put 'em there, came in with flatbeds and took them away. Most of them were destroyed. They burned 'em outside of town. They just couldn't demolish them in-place or they woulda been fined. So they burned on private property somewhere in Williams County," Larry explained.

There was silence as they drove on, turning this way and that way, as Larry pointed out the collapsing infrastructure.

"What happened to the Williston bureaucrats? Do they have a plan?" Wayne asked.

"Ha, those guys left town. Last man standing is Gaylor. He's the Mayor now and doing a pretty ethical job of winding things down. Those other scoundrels took the money and ran," Larry said with disgust. "Ditzy still owns the newspaper. I see her around town every day now. She had to sell off all her horses."

"Your fiancée's dance studio? How's that doing?" Wayne asked.

"Closed it at the end of the December. Lease was up, no business," Larry replied.

"So now what? What's your Plan B?" asked Wayne.

"I ain't got no Plan B. I was hoping you'd convince Cindy to move to Seattle," Larry said, not joking.

Wayne looked at him askew.

"Are you serious?" Wayne asked. "Thought you wanted Hawaii."

"Yes, I'm serious. You got me here, now you gotta get me out of here," Larry laughed.

"Alrighty then. I'll talk-up Seattle with your new wife this weekend. Maybe you guys can take the train back with me. Can she cook? I have an extra bedroom in my apartment. You guys can stay with me a couple months," Wayne said.

"I knew this would work out," Larry said smiling.

Wayne nodded his head, and looked out the window before he spoke.

"We've come full circle."

THE END